Triduum of Death

A Collection of Dark Stories

Airian Eastman

Copy right © Airian Eastman 2020

All rights reserved. No part of this publication may be reproduced, distributed, or transmitted in any form or by any means, including photocopying, recording, or other electronic or mechanical methods, without the prior written permission of the publisher, except in the case of brief quotations embodied in critical reviews and certain other noncommercial uses permitted by copyright law.

This is a work of fiction. Names, characters, businesses, places, events, locales, and incidents are either the products of the author's imagination or used in a fictitious manner. Any resemblance to actual persons, living or dead, or actual events is purely coincidental.

Published by Eastman Books

Cover Design by Airian Eastman

MORE BY AIRIAN EASTMAN

Forever Family
A Kiss for Cadence
Breckenridge Boys
Melody's Song
The Lost Years
James and Cadence – A River Romance

SHORT STORIES
That Summer – Tales of Love and Loss
Triduum of Death – Short Horror Stories
The Bear – Campfire Tales
Among Giants – NY State Tall Tales

CHILDREN'S STORIES
The Niblings
Henric and Vivee Meet the Mountain King

The Sisters
Lila and Ollie Find the Fairies

WITH MICHAEL EASTMAN
Last Light Saga
Death Unbound – Book One
War Unchained – Book Two
Pestilence Unleashed – Book Three
Famine Uncaged – Book Four
Last Light – Book Five

Songs for Triduum of Death

Heaven, We're Already Here – The Maine
Under the Graveyard – Ozzy Osbourn
Demons and Angles – LOWBORN
Bad Guy – Billie Eilish
Insomnia - Daya
Kills You Slowly – The Chainsmokers
Fallen Star (Orchestral Version) – Kamelot
Under Grey Skies – Kamelot
Love You to Death – Kamelot
Ophelia – The Lumineers
Saving Grace – Flyleaf
Close My Eyes Forever – Lita Ford, Ozzy Osbourn
Never Tear Us Apart – INXS
I Will Follow You into the Dark – Death Cab for Cuties
Love You to Death – Type O Negative
Heaven (Little by Little) – Theory of a Deadman
Apologize – Silverstein
Rest in Pieces – Saliva
The Noose – A Perfect Circle
Never for the Damned – Paradise Lost
Fallen Children – Paradise Lost
Erotic Angel – Inkubus Sukkubus
S.O.S (Anything but Love) – Apocalyptica feat. Cristina Scabbia
End of Me – Apocalyptica feat. Gavin Rossdale
Broken Pieces – Apocalyptica feat. Lacey
Arsonist's Lullaby – Hozier
The Reaper – The Chainsmokers, Amy Shark
Whore – In This Moment
The In-Between – In This Moment

Dedicated

To Uncle Babe & Ethan – always the pranksters

&

Jim, Katie, Gary, Tim, Connie, Laurie
and all the other 'Chillers' circa 97-99 for teaching me how to scare!

Contents

Songs for Triduum of Death 4
    Dedicated 5
Preface 7
    My Life 9
Triduum of Death 10
    I could speak 42
Twinkle Little Star 43
Starlight Starbright 49
I See the Moon 54
    Coming Apart 59
Threads 60
Aliens & Demons 70
Darkest Hour 76
    Eyes 81
Royâ 82

Preface

I began writing at the age of ten. It started as a way to clear the thoughts out of my head, and to connect with a grandmother I'd lost at the age of three. I hardly knew her and there were so many questions about her death that I, as a young girl, did not understand.

All throughout school, teachers told me what I should and should not write. I was a depressed and suicidal young woman, and by the time I reached 9th grade that was common knowledge. A poem I wrote, the one which appears at the beginning of this collection, was criticized by the teacher telling me "you cannot possibly believe what you wrote. It's wrong." I disliked that teacher for many reasons. But to tell a student that what they wrote is wrong, when it was written for personal reasons and not part of a class assignment was frustrating. I argued with her and decided from that point I would write what I wanted to write, without letting anyone tell me otherwise. That is when I learned constructive criticism was helpful but criticism was not.

I continued to write stories, ideas, poems, songs, and letters. Totes full of pages and journals collected dust as I went on to the next story.

I took college courses in creative writing and sat in with a famous Ithaca native son, Nick Sagan as he shared with us his own writing and adventures from his Star Trek days. I was fortunate enough to take a class, Advanced Screenplays with his wife Clinnette. I gained amazing insight and mentors during those college years, but still I held myself back. I figured nothing was good enough to share with the world.

The world also had such a negative view on Independent Publishing.

It was in 2013 that I decided I was going to publish a novel my own way and not let anyone tell me otherwise.

When I republished that first novel, a romance, in 2017 I'd met several people who were also jumping on or had been on the indie publishing bandwagon for a while. They all had so many things to tell me, but not all of it was what I wanted to hear.

It is hard when someone tells you to rush a story out just to get it done, that it is about the money not the content of the books. It is harder still when you spend time and money investing in resources from others online only to have them swindle you.

I trusted a woman who went by Trinity. She was the co-owner of Witching Hour Press. I was excited to work with her. She, like so many others, was a fraud. She extorted money from writers and published garbage anthologies in the end. Most of the authors were never compensated. She's still out there trying to make another name for herself and gathering new authors to her cause, which is money in her own pockets.

I share this because it took me most of my adult life to gain the courage to share my work with others. It took a few seconds for someone else to tear down all I'd worked for. Triduum of Death was meant for WHP, as was my husband's debut novel.

The lessons we learned from our dealings with others is that everyone has an opinion and you have to decide for yourself what it is you want.

I have a darker side, a twisted place that I rarely show. Too often I am writing the love stories, fantasy, and fairy tales. While I don't always see happy endings most often I try to leave the reader with something more than they started with. My tales are meant to inspire emotion, good or bad. I've spent my life in the pages of books. I will continue to do so until I'm not able to anymore. I write for one person alone, that is myself.

I share what I write for everyone else, so they may read a story and know they are not alone. That in this crazy world where everyone has a voice and we are all lost among the crowd there is still meaningful work being done. Writing for me will never be about the monetary gains but for the intellectual and emotional ones.

So this is for you, my readers, followers, friends, and family: I will always have a story to tell and do my best to make it worth your time to read it. Thank you for sticking with me on my rollercoaster journey.

My Life

This was the poem which I wrote in 1998 on my own time. During a meeting of the school magazine which would feature poems and stories from the school and community I shared it with a friend and the teacher overheard. She wanted to see the notebook – then proceeded to tell me that 'there was no way I could believe what I just wrote. It was wrong.' For me, this poem was about something more, about empowerment over others. I was torn down so often and so afraid of someone taking choices from me that I had to write about it. This is one of several such poems but was never meant to encourage violence but empower me to rise up.

This is my life and you cannot take it.
Go and stab me with a knife.
See if I die.
Even if you can do so,
I will live on.
And I will let you know that you can never take
My life.

Triduum of Death

This story was originally meant as part of an anthology work. Before the publisher went bust they added in the work in progress version instead of my final version. No one has seen this story completed until now. The inspiration was Scorpio – the birth sign. I based it on the Catholic Allhallowtide, the triduum of All Saint's Eve, All Saint's Day, and All Soul's Day (October 31, November 1-2), with an unusual, dark twist.

1.

Sharing my face with another person frustrated me enough, but to share my mind wore on my nerves. I despised my identical twin. Our likeness ended with the physical. We were born during All Hallowtide, two days apart. Tara was born on Halloween and me on All Souls Day. Our mother labored forty-five hours, the last nine brought me into the world and took her out. The doctor did nothing to save her, though I was often blamed for it.

"Jealousy is not your best trait sister." I heard in my head.

"No one asked you. And who said I am jealous?" I replied aloud, turning away from the window as the dark skies unleashed a torrent upon the city.

"Talking to yourself again. You really must call my therapist." Lena, my assistant entered the room. She was a garish woman. Heavy makeup on her plump face made her look like a delectable fruit that was left too long rotting in the sun. Constant tanning assisted the effect.

"What do you want now?" I asked, straightening a photo on the end table as I passed. Pausing a moment to gaze at the image taken years ago, when Tara and I remained identical. Our platinum blond locks curled around angelic oval faces, thick blond lashes, and full, pouty lips.

"You must be so proud of your sister. She is a huge success. Are you going to attend her homecoming concert?" Lena prattled.

"You're still here?" I forgot why I hired her and racked my brain to recall any redeemable quality about her. Coming up empty I scanned the room, adorned with the finest antique furnishings and impeccable fireplace which I never used.

"I'd love to meet her." Lena dropped hints about my sister.

"I don't follow Tara's music. You must know I have more important things to busy myself with. What did you need?" I asked again, still confused by her initial appearance.

"It's after six. If we review your schedule for the rest of the week I can go home for the night." She made her way to the table in the next room and I followed. For an assistant, she never helped and always wanted to go home. I recalled my early days in the business world. Success was working long hours with little sleep, too much coffee and open ears. You never knew what bit of gossip would come in handy down the road. It was why I now sat at the head of a billion-dollar science and tech corporation leading cutting edge research and development.

I sat across from Lena and studied her bright pink nails with flamingo embellishments. I prefer a clean, classic manicure. Elegant. Perfect for any occasion.

"Tomorrow is testing for Project Triduum. Doctor Windsor will meet you in the morning. I have the latest data here for you. You have a dinner tomorrow night with the head of DIME Industries, Alexander Troy. He's coming alone. I read he just broke up with his fiancé." She whispered the last part as if someone would overhear us, though we were alone in my penthouse apartment.

"Why is she whispering?"

"I've no idea," I answered. Lena must have felt I was talking to her and she continued my schedule.

"Friday is a budget meeting. And you have a charity event on Saturday evening. Your stylist will arrive at noon to assist you."

"Very good. Is that all?"

"Well... I was asked if you had plans for your birthday this year."

"It's not a significant milestone," I recalled turning thirty. I allowed a large party in my honor. This year my birthday would mark a momentous occasion for all humanity. I waved her off.

"If there is nothing else…" I shook my head. Lena left some documents on the table for my review and stood to go.

"Oh, just one more thing. Contact Jane, my sister's manager and find out where she is staying. Once you know have my florist send a large bouquet of blood-red peonies. Just the peonies, none of those little white flowers or greens. Oh and have her add a single Dionaea as well, potted and delivered separately…" I paused at Lena's blank stare. "Dionaea, d-i-o-n-a-e-a. She should know what it is. Just be sure they are sent to her before the concert, on the day she arrives. If I know Tara she will want to make an event of the whole homecoming show."

"Certainly." She left without another word and a sinister shadow crept into my mind. I was never alone, not even with my thoughts it seemed.

"You would be lonely without me. You certainly know how to treat a girl, peonies with a side of flytrap. What are you trying to say?" The voice was clear and crystalline. Distinct. I ignored it and did not bother with an answer. Instead, I poured over the notes left on the table before scooping them up and heading to my office.

2.

I scoured the data for the project and made some calculations and adjustments. After the work was done, I turned on the only TV I owned to the twenty-four-hour state media. It was no surprise that both my sister and I were featured in tonight's headline news. She was wrapping up her North American tour with Liturgy, her metal band.

Father had not been proud of the name, nor her dark music that contradicted our strict, religious upbringing.

Tara dyed her hair pitch, rebelled against schooling, and failed to graduate. Furthermore, she'd used a scorpion for the band's logo. I understand being born on Halloween but did she have to give in to the stereotype?

"Have you spoken with dear old daddy?"

"Not since wife three left him," I answered aloud. "Should be getting a call any day now." It was like Father to come crawling back in between trophy wives.

"Do you think he will take another wife?"

"I don't quite care."

"Perhaps losing Mother broke him."

I brushed off the thought. For a man who took the instructions of the church as sacred and lived by the rules, the one that never seemed to apply was divorce. That sin he had committed twice and was heading to his third. At least he was smart enough to require prenups. Our inheritance from him was safeguarded by the agreements each wife signed, not that I needed the money he would leave. I had earned enough of my own and still found little use for it. My ambitions were on the greater advancement of the human race.

"Kali Wolfgang, CEO of Ratio Technologies refused another call by Congress to appear willingly on behalf of her company. Senate majority leader Nate Keller spoke on her refusal this afternoon. "We have given Ms. Wolfgang plenty of chances to appear and discuss the work of her company, which insiders report is not only dangerous but a waste of taxpayer money."

I scoffed at that comment as Keller droned about my work. I was tired of answering them.

"Her refusal is suspect." The newscast now brought on experts to debate my situation. "Several scientists have gone missing. Her lab is designated top secret and no one is quite sure what she is hiding. It is the reason Congress wants answers." The reporter had a bulbous nose and a ruddy face. His counterpart stood up for me. I liked this guy; he was young and levelheaded. "While the company has several government contracts, the current project under discussion is not funded by taxpayer money. Ms. Wolfgang has been clear on that, and in fact, she has allowed intense scrutiny of her records concerning government funding. What she is doing now, she believes will preserve our future. With a government unwilling to listen to reason about its demise, it is the scientists, billionaire philanthropists, and visionaries who will save us all." I turned the volume down on the TV to review my meeting with Mr. Troy. His technology would pair well with my research and was vital to the next step. Without it, everything I had done was a waste of time. I allowed myself a moment to search the gossip column. Lena was right, his fiancé broke off their engagement.

"Seduction is a great tool. You might try it sometime."

"Whore," I replied. I heard her laughter, sinister and chilling.

3.

I arrived at my office at five-thirty the next morning. The building was quiet but in a few short hours, it would be filled with office staff, scientists, and clients, along with a school tour. Compared to most billion-dollar companies, our building was modest. Three floors laid out like a large high school, with an atrium in the center and a garden on the roof where employees could take lunch. I wished I could take credit for the design and company, however, I inherited it from Walter McGregor. I followed his footsteps and upon his death took over the company.

"How did he die again?"

"I'm not talking to you today. If you can't be quiet at least don't speculate that I had anything to do with it." I muttered. My heels clicked along the lobby floor as I headed straight for the elevator. I pressed the call button and once inside the elevator entered my code, allowing me to access the basement levels. Two lab floors lay below the main building, accessible only to top-level staff.

"You have to talk to me." I cringed as she was right, sometimes there was no avoiding her and today was just such a day. In the lab's outer office I set my bag down, removed the documents, and sat at the main computer. Inputting the numbers now would save time once the staff arrived.

"Good morning, Ms. Wolfgang." Doctor Caleb Windsor greeted me an hour later. "I see you have my notes already input."

"I made a few corrections," I replied, my tone clipped.

"Yikes, a bit frosty this morning, aren't you?" I refrained from answering her aloud, as I so often did when I was alone or in less intelligent company.

"I believe you are right. Those numbers look better than the ones I had. Thank you for taking a second look." He leaned over me and I could smell his cologne, sandalwood, and spice. His ebony skin was rich against my alabaster and not for the first time I felt the sensual pull of lust. It was unprofessional but in another time I would have considered him as more than a subordinate. "I'd like to go over the desired outcome versus the expected one. This will likely fail, after all."

"I do not believe it will fail, though the connection will be short. I believe that we can open a small window into the other realm."

"You will have everything you need for the final test at the end of the month."

"Do you still believe another dimension exists?" Doctor Windsor whispered. His breath warmed my neck. I shivered.

"Of course it's real. Where the hell does he think I am?"

"I would not have spent my entire life's work on this if I did not have a shred of proof. Besides, no one in history has been this close before. We have to believe it will work."

"Can I ask you how you can be so certain? It is not that I doubt you, but the theories you suggest, and the information you have."

"The theories are not my own, you know that. It has been suggested that dimensions can be tapped into if we know the parameters."

"But how do you know them?" Caleb wondered. His legs shook with nervousness as he awaited my answer. I smiled and shrugged.

"I can't give away all my secrets."

"Protecting me, Sister?"

Doctor Windsor accepted that for now, tabling the discussion until after the test. I continued to prepare the setup. The actual lab was a sterile space. I could feel the doubt creep into my brain again. If this didn't work then perhaps I was crazy. It wasn't the first time someone believed their theories to be sound, only to discover the obsession driving them was a tumor or some mental defect.

"Shut up, already. The only mental defect you've ever had is this nagging self-doubt."

"Fine," I said aloud. Several of the scientists around me paused to see if I was speaking to them. I smiled, a polite gesture, which felt unfamiliar. They returned to work.

4.

"Are you ready?" Caleb asked once the staff was in place and the final checks complete. I was not certain I would ever be ready considering we'd only dreamt of this day. I nodded and moved to the head of the room. The office overlooked the sterile lab below, giving us a clear view. Also, it was wired for sound, video, and equipment to monitor nearly every variant we thought necessary.

"This occasion is a day that our predecessor Walter McGregor never imagined. Today we are on the brink of making history. If this works we will have proven the theories of many great scientific and genius minds. Doctor Windsor if you please." The room fell silent, and the lights of the office dimmed, leaving the glow of computer monitors. The screens in the corners of the room lit up with the feed from the lab below. It was empty, we had learned when we tried this several times before, hence the rumors of missing scientists. The experiment proved dangerous because we did not know the parameters to set.

"This will work." She said again, so loud in my mind that I thought we had already made contact.

"Do you know what to say?" I whispered as the final checks and countdown began.

"I know what to do. Trust me, Sister." Without my connection, this would not have been possible, and dialing in the specifics took time.

"Let us hope it's correct this time. No more mistakes." I said as the countdown ended and the room fell silent. We had changed the parameters again, heat, gravity, any tangible, measurable element. We even altered the purity of the air.

We waited; I held my breath… "Sister," I whispered. Nothing happened. Nothing changed. "Damn it." My fist came down on the nearest surface and I cursed, turning my head away from the lab below.

"Ma'am." I heard someone say.

"Look." Another scientist uttered. Gasps and noise filled the room.

"Hello, Kali." I heard the familiar voice and turned my eyes back to the lab. Before me, I could see the air in the lab shimmering and moving.

"Who. Who are you?" Doctor Windsor asked.

"My name is Inanna."

"Check the data, what are we looking at?" I heard from behind me.

"Adjust the nitrogen and try adding white noise." She told me.

"Bring the nitrogen levels up by a half percent. Turn the speakers on and add white noise." I relayed her order.

As the scientists made the changes I stared at the shimmer in the room. It began to darken. As the shimmer coalesced a fuzzy figure began to take shape and sharpen. I watched the cameras, now zeroed into the spot where she stood.

"Am I your first point of contact with another realm?" Her voice was clear, familiar, comforting.

"How is this possible?" Caleb muttered.

"What are we seeing?" I asked.

"Can you see me?" She asked.

"Not well," I confessed. We attempted to clear the image and further improve the connection.

"We're losing it. Damn it."

"We can try again Doctor Windsor." I reminded him. "How long did we have contact?" I asked as the room went silent and all connection was lost.

"Two minutes twelve seconds." A tech replied.

"Not good enough sister. You couldn't even see me."

"We will try again," I said to my sister as much as the room. "In the meantime, I want preliminary reports by noon from all departments with full analysis by next week. Caleb followed me to my office as I left the room.

"Care to venture any guess as to what happened?" I said before I crossed the office and sat on the sofa. The deep red ocher leather was soft as butter. Caleb sat across in a matching chair and relaxed a bit.

"You said yourself dialing in the perfect conditions takes time. It, like any experiment, is bound to have problems. To be honest I was surprised we got that far. When would you like to try again?

"Early next week. Otherwise, we risk missing our deadline."

"Tell me again why you are pushing for this?" He questioned.

"It's a hunch. I think that we stand the best chance for opening the doorway during certain conditions."

"You sure it's not because Halloween and extradimensional portals seem to go hand in hand?" He wondered. I felt a grin spread across my face as I chuckled. "Have dinner with me?" His request blindsided me and I fell silent, gaping at him.

"Um." My instinct said no but what was the harm in agreeing to dinner. "When? I'm meeting Alexander tonight." I gave in, my curiosity piqued.

"I'll set something up with your secretary. She knows your schedule better than you." He laughed. I couldn't argue but fell somber. If he was doing that it was just another professional reason. I had little reason to hope for a personal relationship with him.

After he left I poured over the data I could access as reports poured in from our teams. "What went wrong?" I asked the empty room.

"I'm trying to figure that out myself. You couldn't seem me?"

"You were not clear. We can tell you are a woman but that is all."

"Pity." She fell silent and I sensed her brooding attitude would linger. I ignored her and focused on how to fix the problems at hand.

5.

I left the office late enough to avoid rush hour traffic. Alexander had a flair for the high life. The exuberant restaurant touted small, exquisite bites of food. It felt fake and overhyped.

"Ah, my dear Kali, you made it." He stood and kissed my cheek. "How's Caleb?"

"Alex. He's well. I'm sorry to hear about your recent romantic troubles. How are you holding up?" I asked as we sat down to the semi-private table. The red, black, and gold I attracted the young and beautiful members of the upper crust like moths. The room was full of them, some hovered at the bar while others fluttered from table to table gossiping with friends.

I studied the menu for a moment and set it aside. "Would you like to order the wine or should I?" One thing I knew better than Alex was wine. While he liked to dine in places such as this, he knew nothing of vintage and bouquets.

"Might I suggest the choice pairings presented with the menu tonight?" The waiter asked. It was rare that I allowed anyone to choose my wine pairings but tonight I gave in.

"Fine. Unless you have a preference Alex."

"No. The house choice suites me." He agreed and waved the waiter away. There was no need to order, the tasting menu format meant we would sample the chef's greatest concoctions over the next few hours.

"I'm so glad you agreed to dinner this time. I do hope it won't all be business. After all I'm nursing a broken heart and need a friend right now." Alex laid it on thick as the waiter returned with the wine. When he retreated I sipped my wine and smiled at Alex. He was attractive, but it had long been assumed by men that the only way for a woman to get ahead was in the bedroom. If a woman desired success in the boardroom she'd best be ready to accommodate the men who could put her there. Alex was that kind of man. I'm not that kind of woman.

"Come sister. You can give into carnal pleasures before marriage. Your notion is old fashioned and he's a catch."

"Shush." I hissed. Alex raised an eyebrow at me.

"I will if I must." He grinned. His smile could melt frozen butter in the middle of Antarctica. It was powerful and I realized; not for the first time, that men could use their sexuality for personal gain just as often as women, and to the same ends.

"Let me get business out of the way and we can go from there."

"Do we have to?"

"You are the head of your company. If you humor me I will allow you to grace my arm at my charity ball Saturday."

"I'd have to check my schedule and wouldn't you be my arm candy."

"You're free. I looked into it. If you go with me it will be all pleasure." My voice dripped sweetness as I tried to ooze femininity. Something must have worked as Alex leaned in close.

"You are a tease. Fine. You have my full attention tonight, but Saturday you play by my rules." His fingers grazed my own before traveling up my arm. When he wrapped his fingers around my neck trying to caress I suppressed a shudder and flashed my pearly whites.

"I'm not a tease my dear. Still I have something you should see." I squared my shoulders and reached for the file I had set on the table when I arrive. It contained details of our experiment and what I knew of the machines we would require. I had drawn detailed sketches and calculations, all with Inanna's input.

"What is this for?" He opened the folder as the first dish arrived. He dismissed the waiter with a nod, not taking his eyes off the first page. I eyed the small plate before me. The menu was an ode to fall flavors. Earthy and rustic rainbow beets with apple and fennel topped with a citrus mustard sauce. Regardless of Alex's decision if the rest of dinner were this beautiful I could leave satisfied. I took a bite and closed my eyes as a smile formed on my lips. Food, great food, was a pleasure I gave into without guilt.

"Is something wrong with the beets?" The waiter asked, noting Alex had not sampled his first course.

"What. Oh. Yes. It's fine." He glanced at the plate then up at me. Our eyes connected across the table. He picked up his fork, took a bite and nodded to the waiter. Once alone he found my curious gaze.

"What are you planning?"

"Does it matter?" I wondered. He flipped through the dozen pages stopping in the middle to read something.

"No, but this is remarkable. I've never seen such a concept. I know you are brilliant but I had no idea you knew the inner workings of intricate technology."

"That's because it's not your idea."

"I'm full of surprises. What I must know is if you think it's possible?" He studied the pages over the next few courses. I devoured my meal while he ingested information.

"It could be done."

"Great. I need it by the twentieth."

"Of?"

"October."

"No." He frowned. "It can't be done." I set aside my fork and looked up at him.

"It must be. I have a deadline. The plans rely not only on your technology but science too." We sat in silence, staring each other down. I was known for my cold icy stare. Alex blinked first.

"It will cost a fortune." He said.

"I have the funds."

"Projects will be delayed for yours. I will take a loss."

"I will compensate you. Better yet, put anyone who has a complaint in touch with me and I will see to it that they are satisfied with your work." Our back and forth lasted several minutes though by the end of dinner Alex agreed to take this on.

"You owe me."

"Of course I do." I said as we kissed goodnight. He was going home with a prize, but not the one he wanted. I was happy to go home alone.

6.

"What aren't you telling me?" Caleb came into my office early the next day. He had a stack of papers and coffee for both of us.

"What do you mean?"

"Call me crazy but you're hiding something from me." He set down the contents of his hand on the small table I had at the side of my office. I knew we were in for hours of work but I didn't mind. I left my email opened and crossed to him. I reached for the coffee and took a seat.

"What if I am?"

"Look, I know you hold your cards close but you might consider that I don't just work for you. The scientific endeavors were left in my keeping. I'm on the board of directors. Don't forget I helped keep this project going when the board wanted to shut it down. Trust goes pretty far."

"Yeah, sis. What are you going to tell him?"

"I must confess…" I began then swallowed hard. The lump in my throat was growing. He leaned in anticipating my words. I hated lying but so far I had not told him a lie. I just had not shared all I knew or believed. "I have a silent partner."

"Silent. If you say so."

"You are collaborating with someone?" Caleb asked. I nodded. "And of course you failed to tell the board."

"It's not something I planned to share with them."

"Why not? Don't you think this is pertinent information? When they hear of this…"

"NO." I lunged forward putting my hand over his. "You can't tell them yet." His hard eyes studied me, then softened. "Doctor Wolfgang." He placed his other hand on top of mine sandwiching it between his own. "Kali. I want to trust you."

"Then please. Just a little while longer." I felt the knots in my stomach tighten as I watched him for a sign of understanding. He brought my hand to his lips and planted a sweet kiss on the back of it before releasing me and turning his attention to the plans. I took a few deep breaths to steady myself before I turned my attention to our work.

7.

I needed air. These events were the worst but networking was a must and charity, as my father taught me was vital to a pious life. I made my way to a small balcony on the far side of the ballroom. My heels clicked on the stone, I hated wearing them. The air was cold, welcoming. The noise of the city sounded far away twenty stories below.

I had spent countless hours in my office and at the lab preparing for the addition of technology that should allow us to open more than a window to my sister. She remained quiet all evening. It was a rare day when her running commentary was not in my head.

While my thoughts drifted to work yet again I wondered if I was becoming too obsessed with it all. Sunday was my only day to relax, though tomorrow I would be looking for a new personal assistant. Lena was falling behind in her duties and I would spend my day off trying to compensate.

I tugged at a sleeve; the lace scratched my arm. Much like the heels, formalwear was outside my comfort. My stylist insisted on plunging necklines, and thigh high slits. The only part that felt right was the deep crimson hue.

"There you are." Alex brought me out of my dark thoughts. He was drunk. "I love these parties. Don't you?"

"Not particularly. I much prefer the quiet of my lab."

"I never realized how uptight you are. I know women in positions of power can be, but I'd heard you were down to earth. Do you ever just relax?" Some of his words came out slurred. He stepped closer. I stepped back.

"Maybe we should get you home."

"Oh, now you're speaking my language."

"Not a chance Alex." Another step forward, another step back, into the hard-stone boundary keeping us safe atop the balcony. I was trapped and Alex knew it. He reached out a hand, as I looked into his eyes. They were glossed over and I wondered how many copies of me he saw.

Inanna was still silent which unnerved me as much as Alex's bold gestures. "Alex you need to sleep this off."

"We had a deal, you would accommodate."

"Not like this." I managed to say as his body pressed me further into the stone. He kissed me. His hands roaming my body, grazing along my breasts then to my hips. I stood ramrod straight, eyes squeezed shut and waited until he stopped. It felt like time stopped. Thought stopped. Then Alex stopped. I opened my eyes. He was staring at me. I could see his actions dawning in his eyes.

"Kali. I... I..." He started to stammer as he backed up. I brushed past him.

"Alex I had great respect for you. I never expected you to be the type. I know you are in pain. I know you know loss but if you ever lay a hand on me again I will ruin you. I hope this is the first and last time you've ever let your judgement slide. It is unacceptable and if I find out you have done this to anyone else I will bury you."

I felt the shutter race through me. My teeth began to chatter as all the heat drained from my body. I fled the balcony and the ballroom in a hurry, down to the lobby. As I waited for the car I fought against uncontrollable shivers. I no longer cared how Alex made it home. I slid into the car and sank into the velvety leather. I would deal with this incident Monday morning in the form of a letter from my attorney. There would be no back-room emails, no hidden messages. His transgression was real and I would see to it that it was well documented.

8.

I couldn't sleep that night. Not because of the incident earlier in the evening but because the heavy pulsing in my brain. It was not a normal headache, but as though some thought rattled around in there fighting to get out. I sat up in bed for the fourth time in as many minutes and threw the covers aside.

Nights like this I knew what I needed to do. From a young age if I had racing thoughts and insomnia I would attempt to work through the problem. I ran over a short list of issues, Alex, my sisters, the experiments. I landed on a particular point of the technology. Inanna never revealed why she wanted us to do this and I could not believe it was for our connection alone. She was hiding from me and her lack of comments told me it was yet another example of Inanna 'going dark.' It was a rare occurrence gaining in frequency.

Was our window for this opportunity closing? Would she fade into nothing but a memory if we did not succeed? Did my sister's life depend on me? If I was off base it couldn't have been by much, for she spoke moments later.

"Of course I depend on you."

"Where do you go when I can't hear you?" I spoke to the empty bedroom.

"Wouldn't you like to know!" Inanna bit back. She was in a mood. I pushed out of the bed and crossed to the row of floor to ceiling windows covered by a thin crimson curtain. The lights of the city glowed below me.

My mind wandered to my father. When I had left home for college he was proud that one daughter followed a sensible path. With dual master's degrees in business and science I had a promising future ahead of me. Success hadn't stopped our relationship from remaining strained. Weekly dinners reduced to monthly visits to only a few times a year.

"What answers are you looking for from him?"

I ignored her, pushing her to the back of my mind and prepared an email to send to my father. It was his preferred method of communication. Even after asking if I could meet with him in the coming week I was still restless.

I settled into my home office working on my laptop until well into the early morning. As the pale fingers of early dawn stretched across the sky I drove to the lab.

Sunday, no set staff arrival though later in the day scientists tasked with tracking and monitoring labs would report for brief stints.

It surprised me to see Doctor Windsor's car in the assigned post next to mine. I found him at his desk, head down as he poured over something.

"Couldn't sleep either?" His head snapped up and I wondered if he had fallen asleep. His eyes lit up and a broad smile graced his face.

"Kali. What are you doing here so early?"

"Work I hope. I've had a nagging feeling picking at my brain all night." I confessed. To my surprise Caleb moved back to reveal the plans again. "You too?" I wondered.

"It doesn't add up. I know how it works, in theory." I waited while Caleb gathered up the documents and crossed to me. Together we walked to a conference room. The video data lit up one of the screens while all other figures flashed on the other.

"The entity in question had a brisk tone, all business. And I've compiled a list of features that are distinguishable from the videos. I believe the entity to be feminine. So for now we will refer to the entity as such. Why is she reaching out for contact and why us?"

"Perhaps those are questions we should ask when we reach out again."

"Does your silent partner have any insight." He asked. I rubbed my forehead. There had to be a way to let Caleb in on everything but with the stress from the night before and lack of sleep I was feeling the drain.

"I will see what else I can find out."

We sat together in silence, studying everything. For hours we poured over minute details. No piece of data was too small or insignificant. We analyzed it as only we could do. It was a mutual obsession, the need for answers.

"You're quiet." I said aloud. Of course Caleb thought I was speaking to him. He glanced up.

"I don't have the answer." He said as I heard Inanna reply.

"I was letting you love birds work through the problem. I can't give you everything sister. Sometimes it helps if you think for yourself." Her cruel laughter reverberated through my mind.

"What happened with Alex? Did he agree to build this for us?"

"If he wasn't going to agree before last night, he will now." I sighed.

"What did he do!?" Caleb shot forward in his chair. His hand reached out for mine but I pulled away.

"He tried to make inappropriate advancements. Implied I should give him something for his troubles and he kissed me. Groped me." I explained. "I told him he would hear from my attorney in the morning."

"Are you okay? Do we need to call the police?" The concern in Caleb's voice. "I should strangle him. I respected him."

"I never took him for a slime ball but alcohol can do that to the best of men. I'm certain I should call the police, but they won't charge him for a kiss. It would bring unwanted attention to us all. Let's keep the focus on the science. Andre's rewriting the contract to include a sexual harassment clause and making sure it is all documented. Media will only spin it to sink us before we get started. With Congress watching that's the last we need."

"Kali." He whispered. "What do you need?"

"I'll be all right. It was only a kiss." A sad smile graced Caleb's face and compassion danced in his eyes; with it the small attraction I had felt for him wrapped around me like a warm cocooning lover's embrace. "Doctor Windsor... Caleb." I began. My voice was unsteady.

"Yes?" He asked when I fell silent and did not continue. I wanted to tell him everything. He was the first person who cared about my well-being. He was protective and kind. What happened to me mattered to him. I felt love and I saw a future with him.

Instead I played chicken, balking at my own lack of courage. "Nothing. It's not important." If he was crestfallen his face didn't show it. He was a patient man in the lab, I was certain he could be in life too.

9.

Monday came and went with steady phone calls from Andre, our lead attorney. Alex begging for forgiveness. His attorney asking for changes to the contract and demanding I sign a nondisclosure agreement. And my father called to confirm our plans. The whirlwind from the beginning of the week turned into days of headaches. On Wednesday when I saw Caleb heading my way that I realized we hadn't talked since the lab.

"I'm so sorry. How are you?" I stood and crossed to him.

"We are ready for another test. Do you have time this afternoon?" He asked.

"So soon?"

"No time like the present. I will clear my schedule." I promised. I ignored my sister as she tried to protest and I met our crew in the lab less than an hour later.

"What changes have we made?" I asked.

"We believe there is a quality that we were not aware to consider. The electrical data suggests that this place is charged with higher quantities of electricity." One of the scientists said.

"You mean to say it's..." I tried to work through

"We believe the atmosphere has a higher electrical field. The currents are higher."

"Also there are higher quantities of Neon." Another scientist chimed in.

"What?" I wondered.

"I bet their aurora borealis is phenomenal." A doe eyed intern mused. I waved my hand and the smile on her face vanished. "If they have them." She added before falling silent.

"Let's not worry about that right now." I reminded those gathered. "We need this to work. I want everyone on their toes. Let's make this connection stick so we can see who we are speaking with." As we began our second attempt Inanna remained quiet. The knots in my stomach began spreading to my spine as I stood rooted to the spot, unable to move.

"Doctor Wolfgang?" Caleb said. I blinked and stared at him. They were all waiting on me. I gave a single short nod. Around me movement began as machines came to life. We were quick to obtain the signal. The levels were spot on and the image formed again.

"Well hello again." Inanna said. She came into clear focus and I saw; for the first time, the sister I had never met. The sister who only existed in my mind. The sister who was stillborn on the first day of November when our mother's labor was at its worst.

The room was silent as the eyes darted between my face and Inanna's. I could feel the scrutiny. Did we have the same eyes or was the color slightly off? Was her hair as white blond as my own? The split second dragged on for an eternity before my mind came back in a rush.

"You said your name was Inanna. What do you know of this world? How is it possible we are communicating with you, and for that matter where are you?" I asked. I hoped it was enough to take the focus off our similarities and back on the science.

Doctor Windsor's eyes locked with mine as Inanna began to answer. "I know your world as I know my own. I have a link to your realm. While we are similar, there are vast differences. We have knowledge and understanding which you lack, but you have the technological advances we need." I felt my stomach turning. A cold sweat broke on my brow. On the screen something flashed and drew our attention back to Inanna. She held a detailed sketch in her hand. She quickly flipped to another page and another, until eight in all had appeared. I was thankful we were recording the session. It would allow us to examine the images in detail.

"That was the point, sister." I heard her say, in my head, but this time she looked at me, dead on, a sneer growing on her face. It was unnerving. A tremble shook me as a chill raced up my spine. "Steady now. Don't lose your nerve."

"This is a window." Inanna explained. "We cannot hold it open for long and there is no guarantee we can do this again. You have the means; I pray you find a way." Her words faded at the end as the clarity shifted and she vanished. The room fell silent as the static noise droned on. All eyes turned to me searching for answers.

"I want copies of those schematics on my desk in one hour. Let's review the data. I want detailed reports by the end of the day. Everything from the air temperature at the time of first contact to the color of her sweater." My tone was firm, not harsh. I did not give anyone time to question me, though Caleb felt the need to follow me with his eyes as I left the room.

10.

Once I was in the hallway I felt the wave of nausea rush over me and I ran for the nearest restroom. My head was buzzing as I made my way to the sink and splashed cold water on my face. After, as I walked to my office I could feel their eyes upon me. The conversations, in hushed whispers, called to me. It was as if the entire building heard of Inanna and our likeness.

"Poor sister, always worried about what they think."

"They know I have a twin." I hissed. "Nothing new."

"Ah, but they did not know you had a second sister. Triplets. Daddy's best kept secret. I wasn't even given my own grave." Her voice was cold. I thought of Tara. I needed to talk to her. I should call her today.

"Yes, run off to Tara. What is she going to do for you?" I fell silent. My sister harbored hatred towards our father. She had yet to tell me what had become of him, Tara, or myself in her world, though if I dared a guess it wasn't a happy fate.

"Ms. Wolfgang. Your sister is on the line." My secretary informed me via intercom. I sighed. Leave it to Tara to know I needed to speak with her. I picked up my phone and hit the blinking button.

"Hey, Sister!" Tara exclaimed. "I had a gut feeling I should call you." Tara insisted that we had a deep connection. She called it twinology, saying that our identical biology exceeded normal siblings. "I see you're in the news again."

"You watch the news?" I didn't wait for an answer. "We had a successful test today, though it is not public knowledge."

"You sound so stressed."

"Normal stress is good." I countered. "When are you in town? I asked my assistant to find out but she hasn't gotten back to me yet."

"Well the concert is on your birthday, though not for public knowledge I am having a small gathering on my birthday. I thought we could have dinner on November first, to celebrate."

"My birthday. How quaint."

"I should be free." It was less than a month away but I knew I would always make time for Tara. While she annoyed me with her rebellious ways and her destructive, self-serving behavior, she was still my sister.

"So am I." Inanna said. I sighed.

"Great! Wait until you see my hair. I have crimson streaks now. It's hot. Oh, and I have a new album coming out." Tara went on about the music and her hopes the band would win another Grammy, as if six in two years wasn't an accomplishment in itself.

I spotted Doctor Windsor heading my way. "Sis, I have to let you go." I hung up and motioned for the good Doctor to enter. "What have you got for me?"

"We were able to print them. We don't have the facilities here to do this." He handed over the sheaf of pages. I scanned them. This would require Alex and a larger lab.

"What would you suggest?" I drummed my fingers on the desk waiting for an answer. When he didn't speak I glanced up. "Say it."

"What was that? Did you know, she..." He shook his head in disbelief. "They are all talking. The entire building knows." Windsor stated. I tapped the intercom.

"Yes, Ma'am."

"Send a building wide memo. Attach the policy regarding secret experiments and the ND agreements signed upon hiring. I want to be sure we don't have a leak."

"Tell me what you know or think about all this." Windsor pushed.

"I have a theory. As impossible as it seems."

"I'd like to hear it. Right now any guess is better than nothing. They will talk unless we can figure it out." He said. I heaved a sigh and sat back in my chair.

"Mirror imaging."

"She looks like you because she is you?" He tried to reason through the problem.

"No. She isn't me. I'm me." I brushed my thumb across my nails as I looked over my manicure. "Dimensions exist. It is clear they have knowledge we may not have. They also do not seem to have the same physical conditions in their realm. Perhaps she is hideous. Deformed. Has ailments we have never heard of. Would you rather the first encounter be with a freak or is it somehow easier for us to accept one of our own? If she mirrors us…"

"But why you?" Caleb asked. I shook my head. "Why not one of the scientists or myself. I mean you have a twin so it isn't that strange to see two of you I suppose but do you have an inkling of why she would mirror you?"

"Your guess is as good as mine!" I replied.

"Not good enough." I was dumbfounded. As a scientist, it was our job to question a hypothesis but it wasn't like he had any better answers.

"Although you know why I look like you and he knows you are hiding it."

Doctor Windsor left me to my thoughts and I ignored Inanna's. Over the years it was near impossible to shut her out, but she remained quiet as I spent my afternoon in contemplation of the plans before me.

11.

It was well after dark when I emailed the proposed schematics to Alex. The building was empty but it did not surprise me when Caleb waltzed into my office demanding answers.

"Is she your so-called silent partner? Have you had communications with her prior to our experiments?"

"Only our whole lives." Inanna piped up.

"What are you hiding." He demanded. "What I don't understand is the motive behind this. Why should we help her? Why is she choosing us to do this? If it were only to speak with us, to make contact with us, the window should be sufficient. With the plans this woman, Inanna, sent she is asking for more than contact. This device is for something else. It's been bothering me. Why have us build this? What is it really for?" I watched Doctor Windsor as he spoke, his eyes blazing now with concern. I knew the time had come to tell him. I wasn't certain he would understand.

"I have a theory but you wouldn't believe it if I told you."

"Try." I watched him, his eyes soft and full of concern. I glanced past him at my sterile office. I was driven but I didn't trust well.

"My family story is well documented. But not all of it."

"Everyone has skeletons." He continued to wait and watch me.

"My mother gave birth to triplets; I was the youngest. My sister, Tara was eldest and the second girl, Inanna was stillborn. Mother died as they pulled me from her womb. My father would not acknowledge Inanna. She was buried with our mother in secret without a headstone of her own." I recalled the first time I remembered hearing a voice in my head.

"I was four. Everyone thought I was talking to an imaginary friend. I didn't understand until I was older that hearing voices in your head was frowned upon or outright crazy. Tara knew, but since she didn't hear it she dismissed it as fantasy." Inanna fell silent as I confessed this to Caleb. He reached across the desk and took my hand. His hand was warm and rough, not what I would expect. I felt a rush of heat creeping up my neck. It was lonely at the top.

"She began to talk about things. She knew about my mother's favorite song and the scent of her perfume. Father never spoke of my mother, but when I began asking questions he confirmed what Inanna said. When I first told him Inanna's name he screamed at me. He told me never to speak of her again."

"Why weren't you allowed to talk about her?"

"He blamed me for killing my mother. He blamed Inanna for dying. He said that it made him care." I sighed. I was not often emotional but the pressure behind my eyes meant tears were close behind. "She spoke of where she was. She would not tell me the fate of our family in her realm, but I began to study everything I could. It brought me here."

"Believing your dead sister communicated with you from beyond the grave led you to the greatest scientific discovery, possibly ever. I shouldn't think it possible but how can I deny what we witnessed?" Caleb was being kind. I swallowed down the rising bile and turned my focus back to the schematics. "What does she want?"

"I'm sorry?" I wasn't sure what he was asking.

"So this woman... your sister, does she have a goal? A plan? Why make contact and ask us to do this?" I sank back in my chair, dumbfounded. Inanna had never told me she had a plan; she only ever supported my desire to find a way to reach her. I had to prove that she existed.

"What do you know about your sister? Is she really your sister? Can she be trusted?" His voice held fear and curiosity. It was the scientist's curse to wonder but fear what could happen.

"I'm beginning to wonder. I don't know as much as I thought and she isn't letting me in." The silence dragged on. The ding of an email had me looking at the computer. "Alex responded. He says it will be a tight deadline but with any luck we will have the device by our deadline. He's worried it will cost more than he originally estimated. He's also proposing changes." I would not allow a single change unless we knew what the outcomes could be.

"Of course. By how much?" Caleb wondered. I shrugged. There were no figures included and with our contracts in place it wouldn't matter.

"He can only charge more based on the figures laid out in the contracts. I was careful with this one. Nothing was left to chance." I retired for the evening and skipped the office over the next few days, opting to work from home. The days were slipping by, nearing our birthdays.

"Cancel all engagements this weekend." I instructed Ethan, my new assistant. He was young, motivated, and capable. All the things Lena lacked.

"Shall I give a reason?"

"I will be at the lab all weekend so if you must explain just say work." I instructed as a tapped my pen against the table.

"Does that include your father? He expects you at service this Sunday." I contemplated the answer for a second before shaking my head.

"No. I will still attend him." We were down to the wire. Alex had provided the machinery as requested on time and within budget. I added a bonus to his company for delivery on time. We had run tests to ensure the machines should work.

Alex had requested another meeting to discuss what happened but I denied him. Caleb prepared for the final experiments with our scientists while I buttoned up the details and calculated everything we would need.

"Do you mind telling me what your real plan is?" I asked the room once Ethan left.

"Don't you trust me?"

"I know you like I know myself. What are you hiding?" I asked Inanna but she refused to answer. "If you won't tell me I can scrap the entire thing." I vowed.

"You wouldn't dare. Besides if you don't do it there are hundreds of other scientists working on this now."

"Yes but they aren't your dear sister now are they?"

12.

The next day Caleb came to my office. "I think we have an opportunity to open another window." He shut my door as he entered and sat across from my desk without directive to do so. He was the only person comfortable enough to do so.

"Oh? What purpose would that serve?"

"Yes, do tell."

"We need answers to our questions. I think it is folly to go into this blind. Your sister, if she is that, holds all the cards. She is handing over plans and while all analysis says it is possible in theory, it could be something else. We just do not have enough facts or data to trust her judgement on this. And frankly, Kali, I think you are a bit too close to this to make a sound decision."

"Because you expect I will say no?"

"Because I know so."

"Well you are right. There is no reason to open another window. Not yet." The skepticism on Caleb's face told me he would do it without me so I clarified. "The lab is off limits right now. I want to review everything again. I don't even want to open a window until we can be sure of what we experienced. That it wasn't some forced hallucination or…" I sighed, feeling exacerbated. It could be a huge risk even opening another window."

"I will do it without you." He vowed.

"You won't have a job." I shot back. He was crestfallen. I sighed and dismissed him from my office with a stern warning not to go through with another test.

"I love your faith in me dear sister." Inanna bragged.

"In that you are wrong." I did not explain to her but my distrust for her had grown. If I had my way no more windows, doors or contact would occur outside of my own brain. I couldn't be sure of her plans and Inanna was less than forthcoming. My instinct told me something wasn't right and my instincts were never wrong.

Caleb attempted to revisit the need for further window tests. I denied him. It was my plan to make changes to the modifications last minute, ensuring failure during testing. Inanna was furious with me. We weren't talking.

13.

"Father." I said as he came into the restaurant where we often had breakfast whenever we got together before church."

"Kali." His tone was curt. He didn't smile or reach in for a hug, kiss, or embrace. He sat down and began looking at the menu. I sat in silence and waited for him to set it aside. He was just as brisk with the waitress. "I will have two six and a half minute eggs. The whites should be set but not the yokes. Make sure they are properly salted and light on the pepper. Two slices of whole wheat toast, medium brown, no butter. They should be cut into threes not two. Black coffee."

I ordered my own meal, a veggie omelet, no toast, fresh fruit, and coffee. Only when she was gone did my father speak to me. "How is work?"

"We are doing well. Despite what you might read in the papers." I knew my father followed his daughters. While he didn't agree with Tara's music it mattered to him what legacy we were creating. "Tara is coming in at the end of the week. We are having dinner. You should come."

"No thank you. I will send her a letter as I always do." The conversation turned to his last wife, the divorce, my devotion to work over the Church and why I was not doing my part to find a husband and raise children. That was needed more than whatever silly experiment I was so focused on.

I did not mention Alex or even Caleb and the budding romance. Instead I turned to matters that would infuriate him.

"Do you believe that we have contact with those who have died before us? Do you think spirits in the everlasting light of the Lord can come back to us in any way?" I was not one to talk theology with my father, but I was desperate for some feedback from him.

"The Good Lord works in ways we cannot understand but he does not see the need to talk to the lowly flock when the shepherd can hear him."

"Do you think it's possible that we can reach heaven? That it's possible for another realm?" I tried to continue but my father held up his hand.

"I know your experiments are focused on contacting other dimensions." He said the word with heavy sarcasm. "There is only one earth and one heaven and one hell. Keep up your sins and we know where you will end up." It was the end of the conversation. Our food came and we ate in silence.

I remained the obedient child through the church service but after as he said goodbye I grew bold. "You can't stop me from forgetting Inanna just because you buried her in an unmarked grave. The world will know her and they will know your shame." I turned on my heel and marched to my car as my father stood slack-jawed on the steps of the church.

"Now you defend me when your plans are to sabotage the only proof you have of my existence?"

"They still need to know about you. Even if you don't get you own way all the time." I whispered aloud.

14.

I had not spoken directly to Alex since the incident. He was relentless. In several cryptic voicemails and two dozen emails he demanded I call before he completed the work. I caved. "What's so important Alex?" I quipped.

"What is this being used for?" He demanded.

"None of your business." I replied. "Just do what you're getting paid to do."

"That's not how this works. I just spoke with Caleb…"

"You have no right."

"I do. I was hired by your company. Yes you are funding the project but he has a say."

"And what was it?" Alex did not respond and the silence dragged on. "Don't make me wait all day. I do have a life to prepare for."

"He wouldn't say. He heard my concerns and said he would speak with you. I can't believe you told him."

"You are lucky I didn't tell everyone. If he wants to speak with me then perhaps you should let him. If that is all."

"No." He shouted at me. "That is not all. I will not build this as you've requested. From what I understand of your project it will be catastrophic. No one in the room, or perhaps anywhere in your building will survive should it explode in your face."

"It's not going to explode, Alex. Besides if you understand it so well then you would know what we are doing. It's a simple as opening a door."

"Theoretical science is never that simple." He fired back. I hung up before he said anything else. Caleb was my next call and after lengthy discussion he promised to speak with Alex again.

Tara called me two days before her arrival. The flowers were ordered and our plans were in place. For the first time I was looking forward to her concert. She asked me to stay with her backstage and I agreed.

Inanna felt it would be the best place for the machine but I had no plans of bringing it. To that end I refused to speak to her, as she did not care to share her plans with me I did not care to see them to fruition.

"You will regret this." She vowed.

That evening I received a call from the security at the lab. They wondered if we had any night experiments planned. "What do you mean?"

"We have a sensor going off in the lab three floors down. I have nothing on my paperwork." I cursed myself. Caleb must be trying to breech another window. I told the guard it was fine and I was on my way in for the experiment myself. Inanna cackled with glee. "Does this amuse you?" I wondered. She didn't answer.

15.

I knew something was wrong the moment the elevator doors opened. A computer alarm sounded and the hallway was filled with a light mist. It felt like a humid day or walking through a sprinkler. The moisture clung to my skin. Something was off.

"Caleb?" I called as I approached the lab. It was dark except a faint glow from the lab. "What happened?" I asked, raising my voice but neither Caleb nor Inanna answered. I grew furious with my sister and frustration at Caleb's disobedience. He wasn't in the lab and there was no sign of problems. I shut the computer alarm off. It showed a breach. "Doctor Windsor?" I called out. "What did you do?"

"He's been a very naughty boy dear sister. But what a delicious plaything." Inanna taunted. I walked to the front of the monitoring room and looked down into the lab.

"CALEB!" I shouted as Inanna's vicious laughter echoed in my head. I was moving. My feet pounding the floor. I ran down the hall to the stairs. The hollow thud of footsteps echoed my heartbeats. My hand was shaking as I pressed my thumb to the scanner and entered my passcode. I had to do it twice before the door clicked to open. I pushed it so hard it bounced off the wall. I ran on without glancing back. Ahead of me in the lab Caleb lay on the floor. I glanced at the monitors. He shouldn't have been breathing the air we pumped into the lab. I brought the levels of nitrogen down and pumped in oxygen to even it out.

When the door slide open I rushed to him. My brain was firing off quicker than I could catch up. Caleb's lab coat was stained dark. I started to search for a wound while trying to answer the questions that wouldn't stop. Why was he down here and not in the control room? How was he injured? Was he breathing? What did Inanna do?

I was jolted by a massive electrical charge. I tried to scream and pull away from Caleb but when I opened my eyes Caleb had vanished and the room disappeared. Everything was dark.

16.

The hair on the back of my neck tingled and stood on edge. Trembles of fear wracked my body. A low hum filled the air. It reminded me of an electrical station. As my eyes adjusted I came to see I was not in the dark but the light was strange and dim. It was distant.

I could taste ozone. The smell of a storm without the fresh hint of rain. Yet in the air the same moisture I had felt in the lab. While it did not feel humid the water was all around me.

This place was foreign. I decided to search my surroundings more closely. I could make out massive dark trees behind me. The branches were lit by a red-orange hue reminiscent of neon lights, though I saw no sign of this.

In the distance beyond that a green haze clung to the sky. I was certain the only shelter offered here would be made within the trees themselves. I turned back to the darkness. The hum grew louder and I saw something coming into focus. It was as a window of brilliant cool blue light opened in the dark. It took a second to realize it was looking into the lab. It took another fraction of a second for my brain to comprehend that I was seeing this through Inanna's eyes.

"Can you hear me Inanna?" Caleb's voice rang in my ears. The voice that responded was my own and hers together.

"Doctor Windsor. How nice to see you again? To what do I owe this pleasure?"

"I have questions and you will answer them. I do not know how you communicate with Doctor Wolfgang. I do not know what you tell her but she is not so forthcoming and I hope you will be."

"My dear sister is a fool. You do not strike me as the same. You opened the window by yourself and it appears to be holding. Come, ask me then."

"What are you planning? Why do you need this device and why did you instruct Kali to use it on the second?"

"My you do have questions."

"Oh I have many more." Caleb's voice was harsh, biting. I flinched, or Inanna did, I wasn't certain what was happening to us.

"The device will make this tiny window a gateway. A portal from my realm to yours."

"Why do you seek to leave your place? Are there other realms or only yours?"

"I believe there are three." We said. Caleb asked for further explanation but that question went unanswered. He asked another and another, all geared towards Inanna's plans.

"Doctor Windsor, Caleb. May I call you Caleb?" Our voices dripped with false sweetness.

"No." He spat back.

"Imagine waking up cold and alone and scared. No recollection of how you came to be in this place. A world so vast and strange. Light, sound, air, the very feeling of your skin all changed from moments before. You can recall your entire life but you are now here, trapped all alone. That is how I came to be here. My mother held me in her arms and nursed me, but her food was never enough. Time ticked by. It ate at my mother's sanity. I was born of this place and know nothing else but she… she remembered the light, the feel of the ocean and sand and warmth. She told me about them as I grew. She told me about my sisters. I sought them out. Tara's mind was strong but Kali. Kali was the dutiful daughter and as my baby sister she seemed all too eager to please me.

So I attached myself to Kali and grew strong enough to reach her. I am the whisper in her mind when she thinks she is alone. I am the reason this experiment worked so well and I am the one who will see your realm and ours joined as one."

"Why?"

"BECAUSE I MUST." We screamed. "Now do as I say and make the following adjustments. Then come to the lab so we can talk face to face." I could still think and see and feel but I could also sense Inanna and her emotions. She was furious. Her anger raged as she explained things to Caleb. He obeyed, much to my surprise.

As they waited she told him of her plans. "There are horrors here that your world could only dream of, and sometimes they do. Creatures from this place have graced the pages of some of your most prolific fantasy and horror authors. But even their worst nightmares do not compare to the reality. You have sunlight. You have fresh air and cool breezes. I have experienced some of that through my connection with Kali but I want more. I want freedom. Is that too much to ask?" Our voices turned gloomy. The sadness seeped into me as it overwhelmed her. "You cannot know the hell, the horror, the desolation that is my world. I want a place in the sun with my sisters."

Caleb entered the lab, taking the first reluctant step and pausing to see if he could breathe. They had stabilized the lab in a way that allowed the window to remain open. Caleb stood now before the window. The compassion he always showed for me was written on his face as he looked at my sister.

"You deserve a life here with them but I do not understand what happened to you. You died here. How can you be there instead? How can you be the same Inanna born to their mother? And how could their mother be where you are? None of it makes sense." He was baffled.

I understood what he was missing. I could feel the calculations, the steps we had taken and what or rather where Inanna could be. Impossible or perhaps only improbable.

"Let me out. Convince my sister to use the device."

"What do you mean? I thought Kali was going to."

"NO." We hissed. "She plans to destroy it and me with her. She is going to sabotage it all."

"But why?" Caleb wondered. "We have worked so hard for this. She has spent countless hours not to mention the private funding for this project. What are you planning Inanna? I know Kali and if she does not trust you then neither would I." He stood straighter; the gentleness replaced now by a stern man. "Alex was right." He whispered. He could feel the threat as Inanna's anger became palpable. It lashed out and a streak of energy broke through the window.

Caleb scrambled back. He turned to go as more energy burst through. She was touching his world and he was frightened. He ran for the door as she focused all her energy at him. The blinding flash set off an alarm somewhere above. Caleb fell to the floor in an unmoving heap and through a tiny invisible crack wet rolling mist found a way into our world.

Inanna collapsed at my feet before she could do further damage and the window disappeared. I with it.

17.

"WHAT DID YOU DO!" Inanna's voice shrieked in my head. Her rage was stronger than I'd ever felt, but something between us had shifted. I could still hear her and feel her presence but she felt now like a caged beast.

"You tricked me." She screamed. "You knew all along didn't you." As my own lab came back into focus she was once more only in my head. I had found a way into her mind. It was with this realization that I discovered myself and my true power. Inanna did not control the doorway between us. I did. I always had.

"I was the lonely child reaching out for something and you latched onto it."

"Of course not." She cried out but her voice broke. She was scared now.

"And you should be." I warned. I turned and searched Caleb over again. When I turned him I could see the massive electrical burn on his back.

"Don't forget sister I have more power than you know." Inanna said. She pushed her rage against my own barriers and I felt overwhelmed once more. I was not used to pushing into her mind. It had taxed me and I collapsed next to Caleb as the world went dark once more.

18.

"Kali. Can you hear me?" I heard a familiar voice and then another as hands lifted me.

"Caleb." I said, thinking of him again. I saw the face of my secretary and our head security guard as paramedics wheeled me forward. They shook their heads, eyes sad. He was dead and Inanna was responsible.

At the hospital I was checked over for signs of injury but having found none the doctor opted to keep me for monitoring. The police arrived not long after to inquire about the events. Security footage had malfunctioned in what they could only describe as an electrical accident. They wanted to know what happened and they were opening an investigation into Caleb's death.

So were the Board of Directors. Once the police left my room was filled with members of the Board demanding answers. Until they had them the project was shut down. It would be permanent if they had their way.

Inanna was silence and had been since the lab.

19.

Tara arrived on her birthday and as promised I went to her party, hosted in the mansion of some executive music producer. It was supposed to be a small affair but my sister never did anything small. She beamed when I walked in. "KALI!" She cried. She gave me a rib-crushing hug before leading me around the room introducing me to everyone she thought was important. I ignored the stares and questions.

Caleb's death and the circumstances surrounding it had made the news, as the rumors of a takeover at the Lab loomed. I had not answered calls from Alex or my attorneys nor did I respond to the board. They were all demanding to know where the technology was. As soon as the board left I downloaded all the footage and data I could from the lab. An hour later my clearance had been revoked. I had everything I needed even as my world fell apart.

"So explain this to me? How does he get shocked to death? That's what I want to know." I overheard a group discussing my work. It surprised me to find Alexander Troy discussing my work with such callousness. The others were actors, musicians, and a single social media darling. He was having trouble following along but was quick to spot me.

"Ask her. She should be able to tell you." He swarmed me with a few others but when I declined to comment and rushed away from them only one gave chase. I stopped in a quiet room off the main living area. I sat down in a chair and sighed. I was not alone.

"Not tonight Alex."

"Then when Kali. You are hiding something from us all and dear Caleb paid the price."

"Don't you dare." I spat.

"Pot calling kettle. You are a hypocrite. You would sacrifice anything for your project and your fame. Can't stand being in your sister's spotlight?" His words stung. I did care for Caleb.

"Do you believe in heaven and hell?" I asked him. He gave a noncommittal shrug. "Do you believe in the power of three?"

"Believe in it? I don't know but I have heard the notion. You're changing the subject."

"Hear me out." I said. When he didn't respond I continued. "They got it wrong you know. The power of three is common enough and it makes sense but it is not the zenith of power. To truly tap into metaphysical power you need to multiply it. Triple fold. The true number is nine. You need three sides with three separate points for this to work." I started to explain to him.

"Take for example. Three people born on three major days of power. That is compelling in itself, but then put them in three different locations and think of what you could achieve. The problem is if they are random people without a connection nothing happens." I could see he was curious and I chuckled. "I didn't kill him. Our experiment went wrong and the electrical charge hit him directly in the back. It was enough to knock me out." I stared at him. "Now give me my device." Alex shrugged and handed over the case he had been guarding all night. "Try going after my sister like you did me…" I didn't have to finish. He paled. I found my way home a while later and did not see Tara until the next day.

20.

Inanna was in a mood but remained silent. I had threatened to shut her out if she raised a fuss. She was dangerous.

"I'm so sorry to hear about your work. And that man. Did you know him well?" She wondered. I thought of Caleb and felt tears sting my eyes. I blinked but she noticed. "Oh you were close."

"I might have loved him." I whispered, not for the first time. I had been telling myself that since his death. "They are burying him next week. I've spoken with his family. His mother is a kind woman. Despite hearing from the Board about the circumstances of the death she asked me to say a few words."

"Will you?" Tara asked. I nodded.

"I owe him that much." She reached across the table and took my hand.

"Tell me what it is you are hiding from me. I know you think I won't believe you but I'm your sister. I know when you are lying to me. I can feel it." Tara prompted and would not take no for an answer. So I told my sister about Inanna and our father's dark secrets. I told her about hearing our sister from a young age. She recalled the imaginary friend I had. As I explained how this drove and shaped my life I expected her to laugh but Tara was drawn in and listened with only a few questions and occasional comment.

"I think she is in hell. Not purgatory but actual hell." I finished. "I pushed back and was in her mind for once and what I saw was a nightmare. She is suffering a life that mirrors ours. She is our age, looks like us but she is trapped there."

"What does she want from you?"

"To no longer be trapped. She wanted us to use the lab to open a doorway and bring her through."

"Is that even possible?"

"We believe it is. Caleb and I thought if we put enough energy into the machine we could open a doorway long enough for her to step through. Once we closed it nothing else could enter either way. But if we left it open too long or if we forced too much energy into it we would create a breech. If we tore through the fabric between her world and ours who knows what could happen."

"And you believe she is in hell."

"Father always said there is only heaven, and hell, and earth. Three realms. That's it."

"So she wants to be with us. That's all she was after?"

"I believe so." I lied. Even if Inanna didn't have any plan for a breech before I believed it was in her heart to do so.

Emotional, caring, and full of life when we were calm the three of us had tempers and if someone wronged us they were as good as dead to us. I had thought things over and knew more now of the lessons my father had tried to teach us. Inanna and my mother were trapped in hell. Releasing her on earth would be its own kind of sin.

Out of the three of us it was Tara who was the least sinful. She had a pure heart. She was energetic, full of smiles and prone to laughter and joy. She was happy in her life. She was perfect. I smiled at her and felt the love for my sisters I had not embraced.

If I had we may be on a different path.

"You will be backstage tomorrow night?"

"I wouldn't miss it for all of heaven." I grinned. We fell into light conversation then, catching up on everything we had missed. I felt pity that Inanna could never know this, only able to live vicariously through me.

21.

"You can't do this." Inanna argued with me.

"It is done." I was through arguing with her. I silenced her as I made my way to the car outside. Tara's show would begin in a few hours.

I placed the case in the back seat before instructing the driver on our first stop. When I arrived, Alex was waiting at the curb outside his apartment. He watched us pull up with a look of curiosity that turned to confusion as my window went down.

"Care to join me for a concert?" I asked.

"What?"

"My sister's giving me a backstage tour. I have an extra plus one. I thought you'd want to see the show."

"I can't. I have plans."

"Yeah, I know. I made them. I arranged everything now get in. I won't take no for an answer. Besides it's my birthday." I begged. He relented and climbed in the car. "Relax." I said placing a hand on his knee. "No reason to get worked up. And don't listen to the rumors. I had nothing to do with Caleb's death."

"I'm sure. What's in the case?"

"Some equipment Tara asked for."

"What happened to the device I made?"

"Let's not worry about that tonight. I thought we could put the past behind us and focus on our future." I made idle conversation with Alex as we drove to the stadium. Once there I reintroduced him to Tara. He was smitten with her and she flirted with him, using her sex in a way only she could achieve.

Three identical sisters. Born on three different holy days. We were the epitome of All Hallowtide and tonight it would come full circle.

I left them after the tour and opened the case. I found the device Alex had made for me. It was a perfect prism, with three sides and a base. The tops of each side created three separate points with a small gap between them. This was all to Inanna's plans.

"I beg of you. Don't do this." She said again.

"You set this in motion dear sister. There is no stopping it now." I had figured out the final piece to the puzzle.

"What are you doing?" A crew member asked. I turned and he blushed. "I didn't realize you were Tara's sister. She didn't mention this."

"It's a birthday present. I told her I had a surprise. This is her surprise. The light show will be amazing. Please don't say anything." I batted my eyes and laid a hand on his arm. He smiled and left with a nod.

"See I do know how to use my sexuality dear sister." I gave a short laugh and finished my preparations.

22.

"Let's hear some noise. How are you doing out there?" Tara called to the crowd. Unintelligible shouting came back in a wave of energy. Tara and her band were nearing the end of their first set. I could feel the energy. It was at its pinnacle. "We're gonna do one more song before we take a break. But first I want to introduce you to a special guest tonight. My sister's birthday is today and while we don't share the same date she really is my twin. I'm gonna bring her out for this next song. Kali. Come on out here."

I had been backstage on my phone activating the program and starting the device. Alex's device was working, it was near full charge.

"Come on baby sister don't be shy." She said as I walked out to her. She put her arm around me. "We want to share something with you. Our sister Inanna was born the day between us, making us triplets. She died at birth but she is always in our hearts. On this All Soul's Day we remember her and dedicate this song to her."

The band had been playing a steady beat behind my sister. When she threw her hands into the air the volume increased as the chords of their most popular song began. The crowd was screaming. Beneath it all I could feel the hum that I only felt in Inanna's world. I was ready for this moment. This was what my life was for.

Alex stood watching backstage. Tara was gyrating and headbanging to the music in between screeching vocals. Inanna was crying, begging me to let her go. She would stay in the cage I had created for her. For now I was in control of her and with it the key to all our worlds.

My phone vibrated and I checked it one last time. Everything was set. The only thing left was a catalyst. As Tara came to me, her beloved sister and best friend I wrapped an arm around her shoulder and brandished the sharp knife. In one swift movement, before anyone could realize or stop me I slashed her throat.

Her eyes peered at me with wonder and confusion as her blood gushed. She collapsed in a heap as Inanna wept.

"Why? You are a monster."

"I am the monster you created." I screamed. By the time my words were finished and I pressed the green button on my phone Tara's soul had ascended. Murdered by her sister, reminiscent of Able she was greenlighted to heaven.

The stadium erupted into a cacophony. The music continued as the band missed their leader fall. The screams began from the crowd when they realized what I'd done and the energetic hum from Inanna's world grew stronger.

Behind us light pulsed from Alex's technological advancement, sending lightning flashing towards the sky. Shimmering ripples appeared and grew. The window between our worlds was rendered as three became one.

"I didn't plan this. How... how did you know it could happen. I only wanted to come to you, my sisters and live with you for the time we had left. Did you plan this all along?" Inanna asked. Thought my answering words died on my lips, lost in a world of screams and horror she heard them clear.

"All my life you've ordered me around. Father pushed me away. He said I was a killer. He said I was evil, but you precious Inanna were trapped in Hell for the sin of being dead at birth, an unbaptized soul. Tara was so pure and good, despite her lack of devotion to father or the church. She believed in things I never could. The key was not only three sisters, but the key was three realms and three holy days. The time when the veil is thin. The time of All Hallowtide. A sister in each realm to unleash darkness upon us all." I cackled as lightning split the sky. I could see Inanna's world coalesce and knew both Inanna and Tara were trapped in their realms.

"Behold." My voice echoed as power flowed through me. I heard Inanna's screams. In the sky above a jagged bolt of lightning ripped open a gash as searing light poured through. Onlookers caught staring at it screamed in agony as they went blind. I watched as they turned away, eyes melting.

The second gash of lightning split the ground and from it poured crimson hellfire. Lava flowed, melting everything it touched and from it arose a massive crown of feathers as a bird lifted its head. The black beak snapping open and closed as beady red eyes gazed down. Long plumes of flaming feathers reached out lashing at the screaming horde of fans.

Some stood in stunned horror while others scrambled and ran. The chaos that reigned was glorious and beautiful and terrifying. I could now hear Tara in my mind as she reached out to us. Her words of comfort were for Inanna alone as she cast hate towards me.

"Oh sisters. You should rejoice. We are the Triduum of Death. Through us Heaven and Hell are unleashed on Earth. We can shape this new world. We hold the power now and none can stop us." I spread my arms and twirled in my sister's blood. I felt joy, agony, sorrow, love, hate... all of it flowing from me to Inanna to Tara and back. A complete circle. We were no longer three sisters but one entity. Goddess of Death and Destruction. I felt the power and energy fill my body as I loomed over all those around. I sensed someone behind me and stopped my spinning.

My voice was the voice of three "What are you doing Alex? It's not nice to interrupt us."

"Caleb was right. He said you were not to be trusted. We thought you might try something like this. Well not you, but I knew it was nothing good." He called. I laughed.

"Nothing can stop us now." I promised.

"Wrong. Caleb and I stopped this long ago." He said as he pulled a smaller device from his pocket. "Kill switch." He shouted as he pressed the button. I lunged for him, but too late. Everything went dark.

23.

The stark white prison held three shadows of smoke and ash. When they coalesced the three Goddesses screamed with frustration.

"We were so close." Tara said. Her apple green skin shimmered with starlight.

"That damn mortal." Inanna confirmed. "You should have destroyed him when you had the chance." Her wings, frail as ancient parchment, unfolded behind her.

"Oh sisters." Kali stretched her many arms, arching her back as she moved. "Our time will come again, and soon. This technology is flawed. We will break free."

"But those sisters, the triplets." Inanna mused. "We managed to snare each of them in turn."

"Yes, they were the perfect vessels in the realms. Such weak spirits, easily overcome." Tara agreed.

"I know you loved those bodies but we will find others able to host us. Do not fret, my dears. The fun is only just begun."

The laughter echoed off the sterile walls of their cell. The tale of battle raged for eons. The forces of light and dark, Heaven and Hell, guarded the realm of Earth. Mortals worried about their fate in those three realms, giving little thought to the elders waiting on the edge, always looking for a way in.

Tara, Inanna and Kali, names given to the Goddesses three; bent on destruction, death and rebirth had waited this long. They could wait a bit longer.

I could speak

I could speak

But I wont

I could wish for the rain

But it just won't fall

I could reach for the stars

But to hold them in my hands

Wouldn't mean anything at all

Twinkle Little Star

The Star Trilogy is a three part story told as Twinkle Little Star, Starlight Starbright, and I See the Moon. It was not until I finished the third section that I realized there was so much more to tell. The inspiration for this story was to blend nursery rhymes with Ancient Aliens mythos of the Star People. My husband was watching episodes of the show when I was working on the first part of the story for a science-fiction magazine.

1.

"Sir, Sir are you okay?"
"Where did he come from?"
"Should I call the police?"

The cacophony of sounds was mixed with concerned reactions from people passing by. The man laid upon the hard pavement staring straight into the sky. He did not blink. Nor did he move, not for some time.

While commuters, business folk and tourists all passed by some stopped to lend a hand. Most ignored him. It was some stunt, or he was a bum looking for a handout. Either way it was a cry for attention. He just continued the vague gaze, not appearing to see the world moving around him. When he finally did make a move it was a simple blinking of his eyes, thought it went unnoticed, the original group that had stopped to help had now continued with their daily lives, forgetting about the man lying on the sidewalk in the heart of downtown.

If they had been watching they might have noticed the most peculiar feature of the movement he made, but as they were not watching no one made a fuss. He appeared to be normal, healthy, and attractive. Of an undetermined age, most would call it the beginnings of middle.

His mind kicked in shortly after the blinking began and the first thoughts were 'am I alive?' And 'where am I?' Everything seemed so bright, it hurt his eyes. The world was never this bright was it?

The light glared off buildings as tall as mountains, lined with a reflective metallic or glass surface. It burned his eyes forcing them closed. While in the relative darkness behind his lids he felt the light trying to get in, as if melting through the barrier.

He sat up. His clothes were simple, grey, and slightly fitted. A suit of sorts, but the kind for flying or prisons. He felt neither hot nor cold at the moment, just annoyed with the light.

The memories of his life flooded in and he recalled with some urgency his reason for being here. He had a task and now he was off schedule. The one confusion was how he came to be lying on the street. A crowded, foul smelling street with too much noise and an overabundance of light. He opened his eyes and prayed the light would go out soon enough.

He stood and people moved out of his way, as if he were a criminal or diseased. They did everything they could to avoid contact with the half crazed looking man who had lain upon the sidewalk for hours. Some recalled how, in days gone by a bum would have been dispersed quickly, sent back to the hovels, out of sight of the hard-working folks. Others wondered if budget cuts in the force along with higher rates of crime were to blame for the loiterer.

He knew nothing of the concerns of ordinary people, nor did he care. His only thoughts were on home, yet without direction he could not find his way.

Recalling the last moments before he arrived in the middle of the walk he was filled with great sadness and deep worry. The crash had left him disoriented and this light was a cursed thing. Some fabrication of the people to push away the darkness.

Little good it truly did, lighting up the world. It simply made life frantic, rushed and filled with disillusion. They would learn in time.

He took the steps down the street as people avoided him. Everyone seemed in a hurry but in a primitive way, as the speed of the machines on the road was slower than more conventional means of transport.

He looked to the sky again, but he could see nothing. He continued until he found a quiet place. It was green and filled with life. It was slow here, and he could finally feel the steady beat of the ground beneath him. The pulse of life. Surely once the Star went down he would see the map the heavens laid before him.

He pictured her then. The face of his beloved. The look of fear in her deep crimson eyes as he told her he loved her, one last time. He wondered if she was still out there or if she too had fallen. He watched the sky hoping for some sign.

Shadows deepened as daylight faded from the world. He became hopeful as the first signs of the deep blue blanket covered the pale blue sky.

His hopes were dashed as the lights around the city began to respond automatically to the change from day to night. They twinkled and glimmered and lit the night so that it vanished all together. The sky was a haze of neon feedback. No stars made their home here.

He was lost, in a world of artificial light. In frustration he began to yell, a harrowing unearthly sound. Somewhere nearby others began calling out, asking if someone needed help. He silenced his call and fled. He needed to get out of here, away from the lights. He sought refuge in the shadows but they were few once he left the protective green of the trees.

Each step filled him with fear, for the light was never ending. As he flew through the streets his pace faster than those around him, he drew more attention. People cried out as he crashed into them, pushing them out of his way or shouldering through the ever growing crowd.

No one challenged him, they just parted allowing him passage. Time became a blur as he ran from the light. It continued to harass him, plaguing his every step. He became lost in his quest for darkness. He traveled along roadways constantly lit by blinding headlights, business signs and streetlamps. As the city fell behind it still cast its glare on the sky, blocking all the stars in an orange yellow glow. He finally passed out sometime near dawn as exhaustion overwhelmed him.

When the hellish glowing orb of the sun passed beyond noon he opened his eyes again and cursed the foul thing. Why was it so hard to let the dark have its time? Each thing was supposed to have a place but in this world of falseness and pride it seemed that the light was the only God.

As he followed the hard black ground he became delirious, dreaming of his travels and his love. When night fell he saw only the giant orb of the moon, full and glaring at him. Still the stars did not show.

He saw the last moments that sent him to this abyss.

2.

"We are nearing it now." Her angelic voice filled his ears. She was sitting behind him, with her back against his as they maneuvered their ship. He hadn't realized they were so close. 'Do not make contact,' they were warned before leaving. Only gather any information that would help.

The heads of their people wanted to know why they had lost contact with those stationed on the small planet. All communication had ceased, and all attempts to contact were thwarted by some interference. They simply wanted answers. They began to pass the outer planets. They were nothing like what he expected. He was in complete awe. The smallest of them passed before he could see much of it, but the rest he kept his eyes opened. Shades of browns and red, the giants passed him. The blue of Neptune, the rings of Saturn. There was nothing that could describe this. He felt so lucky they had been chosen for this mission.

"I thought after this we could take a trip somewhere, away from work." She said to him in her sweet tone, breaking his thoughts.

"Pick a planet." He laughed, suggesting they vacation in this system when their work was done. He began checking over the craft as they rounded the grey orb circling their destination below.

This region was known as the Earth System, as the ancient ones had named it. They were told what the Earthlings named their fellow planets but their own set of names worked just as well. The neighboring red planet was ES-4, the fourth planet from the star in the Earth System. Simple, scientific, he had no reason to know it as anything else.

"It is beautiful..." He was cut off by the loud alarm on the board. His attention shifted as he searched for the malfunction. The green light flashed angrily at him as he continued to input a sequence.

"Velocity systems malfunctioning." Her voice echoed in his head as the beeps continued. They had not slowed down as expected. The planet was fast approaching.

"Try the reactor- 010010110 289 0029." He commanded in a sharp voice. He continued to press buttons and input code. They had to slow down, before they lost complete control.

"Not responding." She replied.

"Power reverse, now."

"I did that. Nothing is working."

"Emergency procedure 11047." He yelled at her. "Dammit Ferana now." He hardly spoke to his wife with such anger but their systems were in a catastrophic failure. They had to abort.

"Mayday, Mayday. This is Starship 45110V ES bound. We are experiencing failure in main compartment programming, reactor systems, velocity systems, power systems a, e, and x are down. The trajectory." She stopped and he found what she was looking at. "Correct it." She yelled. He began the process of manual override. He would have to steer the craft himself, something that was only done in extreme cases.

"Trajectory off, atmospheric impact eminent, manual correcting now." Everything seemed to be happening in slow motion though only seconds had passed.

"Command we are going to have an atmospheric breach in 4, 3, 2." She went silent as their craft entered the fiery hell that was Earth's atmospheric cloud. The craft began shaking as the flames burned. The craft was scorching. He did not have the time to correct the trajectory enough, they were falling apart.

"I can't get control." He screamed. "We have to ditch."

"We can't..." She started to argue.

"Ferana, now!"

"Command, procedure X now, ditching over land. Repeat ditching over land. Communications do..."

The impact with something was sudden and unexpected. In their free fall the last thing expected was to crash into something. He hit the eject buttons before his wife could finish speaking. Their seats opened below them shooting them both out of the cab of their craft. It was crashing to the ground with the wreckage of another craft, not of their make. The last thing he saw was his wife, grey in color, unconscious. She looked injured. Then she was gone as he blacked out, the world fading behind his eyes.

3.

Coming back to himself he sat beside a building where happy sounds came. He could see the small earthling children at play. He watched them for a while, thinking of his beloved Ferana and where she might be. He prayed she had survived, but what good was hope when no one could hear you. In this far away planet, foreign and unforgiving he was alone. They didn't even remember the darkness here.

He was sure he would never see the stars again when a voice filled his head. It was beautiful, triggering something deep within his mind.

Twinkle, twinkle little star, how I wonder what you are.
Up above the world so high, like a diamond in the sky.
When the blazing sun is gone when he nothing shines upon.
Then you show your little light, twinkle, twinkle all the night.
Then the traveler in the dark, thanks you for your tiny spark.
He could not see which way to go if you did not twinkle so.

He found himself following the voice until he stood staring at the child singing. He had understood the words, spoken in his own language. The little Earth-one began to run off.
"Twinkle. Twinkle."
The child stopped and turned to him. "Little Star."
"Little Star." He nodded and pointed up. The child held out their hands and formed a symbol. Two fingers pointed up, two down. He looked to the heavens then the sandy ground below. He had very little training in EA-3 languages, he was never meant to make contact. He was not even certain how he understood this one.
"Show, little star." He said. The child pointed up, speaking again.
"They will show you the way." The expression was of excitement, and that the stars were there. He did not know where for certain but he had to follow the child. Just then a large Earthling began to approach. He moved back away from the little one and watched from the shadows. He waited. How did the small one understand his words? When the sun was almost gone the child emerged from the building again.
He followed the movement of the little one with a large one, they went to one of the metal machines. Following them, he was able to climb in the back, a flat open spot, when they were not looking. He laid down and kept watching the sky as they moved away from the lights of the town. The air was dry and warm, it had been very hot but now it was cooling fast. He waited until they stopped moving some time later. Then he climbed out. The light here was darker, and with the sun now behind the sandy hills he could see the first twinkle of the stars.
They were there, above him, just as the child had said. He was the traveler waiting for help.
He watched as night deepened and the stars began to shine brighter. He stood in the yard of the little one, not thinking of the Earth people. He did not see the large Earthling approach him, until they stood face to face. He looked at the stranger and saw something familiar in his eyes. The slight slant, the strange blink, not like a human. This was one of his people.

He looked at the Earth stranger and then at the sky. As he looked at the stars the stark truth came back to him. For now this was his home. For now he was as lost as the rest of his people, forgotten on a planet abandoned by the ancient ones. He felt numb as a hand on his shoulder turned him towards the dwelling.

"Welcome home, Traveler."

Starlight Starbright

1.

"Sir. Sir, you need to see this." An advisor handed the report to the Secretary of Defense. General Brisk was a brutal man, known to lead with iron and steel. The nation was on the verge of war and the enemy could strike at any moment.

He glanced at the report before shouting commands. "I want eyes in the sky. Find out if it was a missile. Get in touch with the SWT, I want to know what flight was hit. This occurred twenty minutes ago we need to know who knows. Get me NorCom. Not a word is leaked to anyone. If you do I will try you with treason. This is a matter of National Security, people. I don't need to remind you what is on the line if we fail."

A phone rang, interrupting his speech. Nearby a frightened young woman reached for it with a shaking hand. She whispered into the phone. When she hung up all eyes were on her.

"That... that was Director Kelson. He needs to see you immediately."

"What does that SOB want." Lee Kelson used to work for NASA but had switched to a private company in search of life elsewhere. Not only did they track the skies for all signs of extraterrestrial life, but he was working with billionaire Maxwell Grayson to fund the first commercial space flights. The world was changing. The stars were no longer out of reach.

"Let's get to work." Frank Brisk shouted before stalking from the room. As a Major General he was the most highly decorated officer to then serve as SecDef.

He went to his office to find Lee already waiting, tablet in hand. How had he gotten the jump on this story? The light on his phone was also blinking. He held up a hand to Kelson and answered the phone.

"Brisk here. Yeah. Well I need answers. Get them there." He hung up and turned his attention to Lee, who approached the desk and extended a hand.

"Lee now is not a good time to tell me how we should be spending more of the defense budget on-"

Lee held up a hand and interrupted him "I'm not here about that. I know about the crash."

"Now how did you find out about that. It hasn't been a full hour and already..."

"You need to listen to this." Lee began punching things into the tablet. "This was forwarded from our home office in Arizona. They picked it up before the crash."

He set the tablet on the desk. It showed a scan of the inner planets. Moving quickly in the direction of Earth an object highlighted in red. It entered the earth's atmosphere.

"Are you telling me this was a meteorite?" Brisk said.

"No." He reached across the desk and brought up another program. "This was recorded at the same time."

They both listened to the conversation, two voices, one male, one possibly female. When compared with the video of the object it was not until after entering the atmosphere that the talking stopped. At the same time as a loud crashing sound.

"That hit my plane?"

"I believe so sir. It is no coincidence. We need to see that wreckage. We may be dealing with something else entirely." Brisk stood and picked up his phone.

"Get me the president. I'm heading to Arizona."

2.

The first responders on the scene of the crash were certain they would not find any survivors. It was a twisted wreck of metal and bodies. The bulk of the plane crashed a mile away, but debris spread across the dry desert sand. In the distance the Phoenix skyline glimmered in the sun.

It was by chance they stumbled over the woman, wearing a skintight grey suit, her face covered by a mask. The EMTs exchanged a hesitant glance before checking for signs of life.

"We've got a live one. Get a gurney." The younger man cried out as his superior began attending to the woman. All care was taken to strap her to the backboard, secure her neck, spine and airway and transport her to the local hospital. No other survivors were found.

"Just the one." Brisk asked upon arrival.

"Yes sir. She was taken to a nearby hospital. I've been told that there is something you need to see." The General followed an officer, Kelson hot on their heels. "We can't explain this." He pointed to the tent guarded by armed men.

"They work quickly."

"Have to when national security is at risk." Brisk responded. "You have secure labs nearby?"

"Of course I can put them on standby." He reached for his phone but Brisk shook his head, motioning for Kelson to follow him first. They entered as someone snapped on floodlights. Before them, in a large crater was the mostly intact remains of a black craft.

"What is that?" Brisk exclaimed when his eyes adjusted to the light. Kelson had shot forward, kneeling towards the wreckage.

"Look at the color, it's as if someone carved this from volcanic rock. I've never seen anything like it." The black material was metal, not stone. It had the sheen of glass and absorbed the light. An hour passed of examining the material, first from a distance, they concluded it was not radioactive, then closer, with gloves and suit.

"You said only a single body was found nearby?" Kelson asked as he left the tent to speak with Brisk.

"Yes. I've got to get to the hospital to question her why?"

"There should be another one. A pilot perhaps. The machine is designed for two and I believe two are needed to operate it properly."

"Damn." Brisk cursed. They climbed into the waiting Humvee and raced towards the hospital where the survivor had been placed in isolation. The reports from the lead doctor were promising but vague.

"We could perform an autopsy." He explained, while leading Brisk and Kelson down the narrow basement hallway.

"I thought the specimen was alive." Kelson stated.

"She is. But we can still cut her open, see how she responds to pain and how her body works."

"You say she. It's a woman?"

"By all counts yes. We were surprised to find she is not much different from us at first glance. The eyes aren't lidded like ours and their chemical makeup, while similar is more oxygen rich. Her lungs were clear, pristine, not what we would expect from someone her age if born here on earth."

"You are saying you believe she is alien?" Brisk scoffed.

"Don't you?" The doctor questioned. He stopped at the door leading to the morgue's autopsy room. There on a gurney hooked up to every possible monitor was the creature in question.

"Oh my." Kelson gasped. He'd never expected this day to come, no matter how he'd hoped for it. He looked over the charts and printouts. "I would have thought she'd sustain more severe injuries. There are no broken bones, no tissue damage. How is this possible?"

"It's not. We have no medical explanation at this time." Kelson looked from the doctor to Brisk who was studying the woman.

Though she had been found in a suit of sorts they had removed it for a plain gown. The woman's hair was short, cut close to her head but still feminine. The color could only be described as chartreuse.

"It's natural."

"That's not possible." Kelson reached out to touch her hair. It felt as soft as a feather. "Unless." He began thinking of what else could be different about this creature. "We should get her to a more secure location, General."

"I agree." Brisk stated, then stepped into the hallway to make a few calls. Kelson knelt over the woman. "Did you give her anything to keep her sedated."

"It's all in the file." The doctor handed over his notes and left the room, knowing he would no longer be a part of this unique investigation.

3.

    Brisk left Kelson at the secure location. Engineers and scientists of all types were studying the wreckage and suit found with the woman while a constant stream of biologists and chemists worked out a DNA profile for the alien woman. She was heavily sedated when they arrived but Kelson believed should wake her. His suggestion was being met with red tape at every turn. He hated bureaucracy ruling science.

    The hours turned to days of waiting. Kelson and his trusted colleagues took matters into their own hands. Dr. Roslin, Anderson and Javir assisted in many of the experiments on the subject.

    The paperwork stated they were performing additional rounds of testing. After all the DNA structure was extraordinary, the fundamental building blocks were the same but her makeup was more complex in many ways.

    "We are not alone in the universe, now we need to know if she can understand us." Kelson told the others. They agreed.

    "The suit and craft saved her life. It is meant to withstand impacts and sudden stopping using the gel like substance they found." Dr. Roslin spoke up. She was a leading trauma specialist developing lifesaving technology for soldiers in war zones.

    "Lucky for us." Kelson lowered the dose of sedative an hour ago. They watched from behind a glass wall as fingers twitched and eyelids fluttered.

    "Can you hear us?" They asked every time a new movement was observed. This was broadcast in several languages. The clock ticked, the only noise in the room as they waited.

    The alien gasped for breath, coughed, and began screaming. Kelson was prepared for this and spoke in a calm manner telling the creature she was stable. At the same time he administered a mild anti-anxiety medication which they felt would have no negative effect on her system.

    The screaming ceased and the figure sat up. Her movements were foreign, fluid and dance like in their gracefulness.

    "Can you understand me?" He asked again. She spoke then, but the language was not one they recognized.

    "Run it through the translator." He barked. Inside the room the woman startled at the tenor of his voice. He'd left the microphone open. "Shit. Sorry. We don't understand you." he spoke again, filtering it through the most common languages on Earth. She did not respond to any of them.

    "Kelson. You're not going to believe this." Dr. Roslin stood before the computer staring in disbelief.

    "What?" He peered over her shoulder.

    "The root language is that of a modern tribe in the middle of Mexico. They are said to be descendants of the Mayans."

"Who do we know in the BTA or Mexican First Nations? Get me Brink." Kelson shouted orders as the woman rocked on the stretcher fearful of the flurry movement around her room.

"She's been repeating that for over an hour." Dr. Roslin told Kelson when he returned from his call with the Secretary of Defense. "How angry is Brisk."

"He spoke of court martial and jail time. Dark holes where no one sees you again. The usual doom and gloom." Kelson shrugged. He ran a hand through his hair and sighed. "Do we know what that is yet?"

"We have an expert on the way." Roslin frowned, staring at the screen before her. "It's a song. A poem perhaps."

"Star light, star bright." A deep tenor said the words.

"First star I see tonight." Dr. Roslin looked up as Kelson turned to see who had spoken. The man had deep tanned skin and soulful grey eyes. Half his scalp was bald and tattooed. The other half rich chestnut hair flowed. He wore jeans and a flannel.

"Doctors, this is Gabor Kukulkan." Anderson, their colleague introduced them.

"Pleasure to meet you." Kelson held out a hand, which Gabor took. "You believe this is the wish poem?"

"Not quite. While the modern version is about wishing upon a star that is not what she is saying."

"So what is it?" Anderson asked.

"Starlight. Starbright. With your blessing we take flight. Soon to have Earth in sight and with our people reunite."

"That doesn't make any sense." Kelson scoffed.

"Not to you, but to my people it is part of our mythos. You see your so-called nursery rhymes are part of our core belief." Gabor looked at the woman inside the plexiglass room. She had stopped speaking and peered at him with a knowing gaze. She spoke a few more words and Gabor smiled.

"What did she say?"

"She said her name is Ferana." He looked at the green haired alien with a soft smile. She stared at him in awe and spoke to him again.

I See the Moon

1.

"No one gave you permission to bring in any experts without my authority. That said it seems the President is interested in communicating with her."

"She's coming here?" Kelson asked.

"No of course not. We can't risk that. She's sending the Vice President and a few advisors. She will be on a secure line back in Washington." Brisk informed the scientist. "And I don't need to tell you what's riding on this. Don't do anything again without speaking to us first. There is a reason we are in charge."

"Yes sir." Kelson cringed. He hated sucking up to military or political men of any kind. He was a man of science; it should have counted for a whole lot more.

Since their first contact with Ferana and learning her name he'd hired Gabor Kukulkan to stay on and act as interpreter. His grievance with how Ferana was being housed was a roadblock but Dr. Roslin had negotiated and now Ferana was in a secure suite. While the scientists insisted on full gear, they allowed Gabor into her suite to speak with her.

As such, he had a rapport with her. They trusted Gabor as he was the only one able to translate with accuracy what she said. Still Kelson felt the man might be hiding something. At the least he harbored a grudge that someone he appeared to revere would be held captive.

"Good morning Director Kelson." Gabor greeted him as he was leaving the decontamination room.

"Good morning. How is she today? Are you getting anywhere?"

"It is slow. I have a few things to attend to in my village but I will return within a day or two." He had not informed Kelson of this.

"Warning would be nice.."

"I have a life outside of this place and it demands my attention. I explained this to Anderson. I'm sorry. I will return." Gabor strode off before Kelson could mention the upcoming visit.

"Shit." He muttered before heading off to meet his colleagues.

Gabor waited until Kelson was out of sight before slipping into his room. He knew that everything was monitored in this place and while the scientists did not know the language well, they had enough software to form rudimentary translations.

Gabor wasn't the only expert either. He had to get in touch with his people. This morning's conversation with Ferana revealed she was not alone. There was much work to be done. He slipped the recording device from his pocket into a day bag, threw in his cell phone and clothes, along with his journal and grabbed his keys. He had to get off this base.

Walking like a man with a purpose but not causing alarm was difficult as he neared his truck. Soldiers and scientists knew who he was and greeted him, but no one stopped him. He did not breathe a sigh of relief until he was a mile from the encampment, heading towards the open roads.

He punched in a phone number and hit speaker. His truck was too old for fancy technology. "Gabor? Where have you been?" His sister sounded worried. He'd been told not to reveal anything. "I thought you'd be gone a day or two at most."

"Colel, I know but listen the most extraordinary event has occurred." He told his sister what he could about it, speaking in their tongue in case somehow someone was listening. "I've got to get to Ian. He will know what to do." He mentioned the other language expert and his dear friend in haste. Ian could do what Gabor could. They had to be on the same page. "There is something else, something I need you to do for me." He gave her instructions then sent a text to Ian asking him to meet halfway. Ian's reply within two minutes was rare. So was the message. Gabor hit the pedal, urging his truck to top speed.

An hour later he pulled into the little known diner and spotted his friend. Ian stood outside the Jeep. Someone remained in the front passenger seat. Gabor didn't move while his truck ticked, cooling down from the race to get here. He rolled down his window.

"I thought I said alone."

"Trust me. You need to meet him."

2.

Gabor stared at Zaden, who had just finished telling his version of Ferana's story. They'd arrived together in a star craft and crashed into a plane when their own ship malfunctioned. They weren't supposed to enter the atmosphere.

"How is Ferana?" He asked again.

"As well as can be. They've run a number of tests on her and more every day but they have kept her alive. I'm afraid once the Presidential group is gone Brisk will terminate." He looked at Ian when he said it, fearing Zaden's disappointment.

"Can anything be done?"

"I've been speaking with her in code, she's marvelously brilliant. She gave me something that she thought would help. Colel is working on that as we speak." He stirred his coffee for the tenth time but still did not take a sip. It had gone cold while he listened.

"What do we do now?" Ian asked.

"I must see her." Zaden insisted but both the other men shook their heads. It was too dangerous. Having one such creature was luck, two would make the other expendable. They told him as much.

"I'm keeping her safe. She said when I saw you to tell you something." It was all Gabon could give to him. "She said I see the moon."

"And the moon sees me." Zaden responded. He gave a nod and left with Ian though Gabon could tell he didn't want to. He'd asked how to free Ferana and Gabon promised when they met again she would return with him. He drove back towards his village then, buying himself a little more time to plan.

"I did what you asked." Colel stated when Gabon entered her house. He knew it would be safer than his own. He never trusted in governments all that much, but now had less reason to. "Want to tell me why SETI is broadcasting a poem?"

"No. I don't want you involved."

"I'm already involved. You think they won't trace this back to me?" Colel shook her head. "You brought me into it so tell me what it is that is going on." Gabor realized she wouldn't take no for an answer so he explained the entire thing to her, from first meeting Ferana to just meeting Zaden.

"So what are you saying?"

"The stories are true. The star people are real. They travel here trying to reach us but until now they thought we'd all vanished." Gabor was torn between excitement and fear. He hoped he'd chosen the right side. After all, being on the wrong side of this point in history would prove disastrous for all.

3.

Director Kelson greeted the Vice President and the advisors when they arrived. He showed them around the facility and took them to a conference room. Though Gabor was back Anderson had secured Ian Xicara and another colleague to assist in the translation. Gabor had agreed to sit with the vice president and confirm translations.

Gabor was already in the room when Kelson entered with the delegates. The window looked into another room where Ian and his partner would meet with the alien woman.

"Before we get started," Vice President Masey spoke after introductions were made and Madam President was brought in via secure video link. "I'd like to ask what you can tell us about the recent conversations you've had with our alien, Mr. Kukulkan."

"Everything we spoke about is in the report."

"Is it?" VP Masey looked to his left and an aide pulled out a file, along with a tablet. "How come SETI has been active in recent days?"

"What are you talking about?" Director Kelson demanded. Instead of speaking the VP nodded and his aide brought up a file on the tablet.

"They began to broadcast a repeating message to coordinates at the edge of our solar system." The aide hit play as he spoke. Everyone listened.

Twinkle Twinkle Little Star, Starlight Starbright, I See the Moon. We have made contact. Send help.

"It repeats in your language Mr. Kukulkan, care to explain how that can be?" Masey stared at Gabor. Gabor returned the gaze. Neither budged. Kelson stepped up.

"What does it matter what SETI is broadcasting? Can we get on with this?"

"It matters, Director Kelson, because twenty minutes ago they received an answer." The President answered from Washington. "It matters because we are no longer alone in the universe, and we just gave them directions and reason to visit."

"What was the message?" Gabor asked.

"We don't know. However I'm certain our resident Alien knows. Why don't we ask her. And let's not lie, shall we?" Masey's tone was clipped. Gabor knew they would not hesitate to harm her or others. Gabor stood and went to the window. He opened the comlink to the room. Ian and Zaden looked up from the conversation they were having with Ferana.

"Are you ready for us?" Ian asked.

"It appears we have a message we need Ferana to translate. Please tell her that accuracy is key." Gabor listened as Zaden spoke to Ferana instead of Ian. Then the message played on the speakers. A flurry of conversation continued between the two. Ian looked at Gabor, wide eyed. Gabor nodded.

"It says, 'Message received. We are coming to you.'" Gabor translated. "It also says that if any harm should befall their travelers it will be met as an act of aggression. They do not wish for that."

When Gabor finished speaking there was a moment of silence before the room erupted into chaos. Everyone shouted at each other, throwing out thoughts, questions, answers, and opinions. Gabor leaned against the glass and peered at his friend. They were in trouble now.

An alarm rang out silencing the room again.

"What was that?" VP Masey asked.

"That signals a detection of an object nearing our moon."

"But. That's impossible." Director Kelson sat down hard in his chair. "They couldn't have reached Earth in that short a time. It's been an hour, at most."

"You are a scientist. You should believe in the impossible." Gabor muttered. As the President demanded someone get Brisk on the phone another phone rang into the room. Anderson reached it first and answered. His face paled as he listened.

"I want to blow them out of the sky." The President said as Anderson hung up.

"I'd wait to give that order." He sputtered. "We have images from the moon base now." He crossed to the table, his hands shaking as he reached for the keyboard and punched in a code. It brought up a live video feed from the moon.

"Oh. My." Masey said.

"May God help us all." The president replied. There on the screen a crystal clear image of Earth, blue, green, brown, and white in its perfection. A semi-circle of ships, gleaming in the solar sunlight filled the remainder of the screen. Earth was under siege…

… *to be continued.*

Coming Apart

They tell me to open up my soul and let somebody in

But every time I do they spit and shit and grin

They try to take back words they weren't meant to say

They try to turn back time like it was yesterday

'I love you' is just three little words I don't want to har

Take them back, keep them, and instill a little fear.

Go on with your life, find a hussy, settle down

Just get your ass out of my town.

Fuck off, but when you do it have a little fun

For after you do it, all is said and done

Then she will go off, leaving your ass behind.

Screwing with your life and messing with your mind.

Now don't take these words to heart

Or you just may come apart.

Threads

My first introduction to bizarro fiction was reading Clockwork Girl by Athena Villaverde. As a fan of steampunk we picked up the book on a whim. I was transfixed by the strange, macabre, and somewhat terrifying stories. I knew it was something I had to try. At the time I was working in a factory (my first and only attempt at manufacturing work). The company used machines to braid threads into rope. It was working the second shift lines when this story began to form.

Mei

Mei Setsuko had no choice but to take a factory job when she arrived in the small hamlet of Olympia. It was the only place willing to hire an immigrant college dropout. Her mother lay home dying of disease, most days she didn't know where she was. Mei's contribution to pay the bills had to be made somehow.

The factory had two buildings, one for filament and the other for thread. It was in the second building Mei found herself on the first day of the job. She would be working an overnight shift while her younger sister stayed home with their mother.

She was introduced to her coworkers by the foreman, Dan, a formidable man with a leering gaze and snide smile. She was the only female in this building, though they told her a few others worked in filament.

"Tommy, why don't you show her the ropes." Dan laughed. Tommy was about Mei's age and like her he remained quiet until spoken to.

"It's a joke he likes to make." Tommy explained once Dan left them alone. They spent the next few hours going over the way to thread the machines and coil the finished ropes into the boxes. Mei thought it was a straightforward job but not without dangers.

"This is where the cast offs, scraps and unusable material goes." Tommy showed her the pit in the back corner of the factory. It was dark here. Overhead the lights flickered. They stood on a ledge looking down into the tangled mess. Mei shivered as she spotted a spider making a web in the casing of the light.

"Just let me know if you have anything to bring back here. I will take care of it for you." Tommy's offer was laced with a warning.

Mei's first week blended into her second and third. She picked up on the machines, her tiny fingers adept at grasping gossamer strands and weaving them into the braids. She avoided the pit as much as she avoided the men. During mealtime she would sit with Tommy at the end of the breakroom avoiding the gaze from Dan and the others down the line.

No one bothered her but their lingering stares and snickering made her uncomfortable. Without Tommy she may have asked for a transfer to the other building or quit all together.

Autumn turned to winter and her mother caught a nasty bug forcing Mei to miss a few days of work.

"She's getting worse." Kiko, who preferred to be called Jenny, informed her.

"I know but she is refusing to see the doctor. What would you have me do?" Mei asked. They had a nurse aide once a day to help, but until Ms. Setsuko could not refuse; they indulged her. Jenny stayed with her boyfriend, an older man from the nearby city, every chance she got, though Mei tried to reason with her that he was nothing but trouble.

The night before returning to work Mei and Jenny argued over him.

"You are just jealous that I can find me a man and you are going to die old and alone like mama." Jenny spat.

"Mom worked hard to give us all we have."

"My life is miserable. I wish she would die so I could move out. You can go back to doing whatever it is you do." Jenny slammed the bedroom door, rousing their mother from her fevered slumber.

"Mei." She heard her mother's weak voice from the next room. Sighing she attended to her mother. Jenny was never going to be anything but the spoiled pretty girl. Mei would always be second fiddle to her.

Mei – A Few Days Later

"Welcome back." Dan greeted Mei as she waited to punch in the following night. Usually she would wait with Tommy but she'd seen his car at the other building when she walked in. He must be covering for someone, she figured.

"Thanks." She squeaked. Not wishing to start a conversation with any of the men waiting around she punched in, set her card in a free slot on the side and found her way to her station.

She put her head down and focused on her line for the first few hours, unaware of those around her. At the end of her line her box of scraps became a dumping ground for three other workers, filling it to the brim when she went to cast aside her own trimmings.

Tommy was not around to help her. She waited until dinner when the men headed for the break room before lifting the first of two boxes. The second she would need to handcart to move.

The factory was noisy all the time, with the drone of the machines and hum of fluorescent lights. Footfalls were silent here. She neared the pit with its flashing fluorescent light overhead, more dim from the presence of thick webs. The spider had been busy.

She did not hear the men approach her until it was too late. Casting the contents of her box into the pit she turned to find three of them blocking her exits, one was fat and bald. She never could remember his name. Dan and two others stood before her.

"Seems Tommy isn't here to do the heavy lifting. Need a hand?" Dan chuckled.

"I. I've got it." Mei replied. She felt bile sting her throat as one of the men reached out a hand, brushing it along her arm as he took the empty box.

"Really, you should let us help. A girl like you could use friends like us." Floyd stated.

"No. I. I'm…" Mei was going to say she was fine but the words died in her throat as her mouth went dry. These men were dangerous and used to getting their way. In the small town no one ever told them no, from women they picked up at the bars to pretty little girls in the wrong place at the wrong time.

"So what are you, Chinese?" Ned's deep laughter echoed off the walls around the pit as one of the men she'd never spoken to asked about her looks.

"Never had Asian but I'd love to try." Pat harassed her. It was clear what their intentions were. Mei tried not to panic. She knew that the pit had a ladder on the other side. If she could climb up she could sneak out the back door and run. She'd have one chance.

She turned and lunged for the pit, hoping to fling herself far enough across. The men were expecting something like that. Large dirty hands reached out, grasping her. They caught her and hauled her backwards, her toes scraping the ground as she struggled to get free. The men were stronger, lifting her like a ragdoll. They threw her down on a nearby work bench.

She was dizzy from the movement and sounds, but most of all from the fear. Dan stood over her peering down.

"We know your kind. You pretty girls come in here and think you can keep up with the men. Damn foreigners take jobs from those of us who've lived here our whole lives." Men laughed as the sounds of clothes being torn from her body and her fearful whimpers were drowned out by the noise of the factory.

Mei was a smart girl. She knew what was going to happen next. Her nana had taught her much of the ways of the world, stating Mei's mother's careless nature burdened her with two children and no husband in the first place.

She could still see the dim light swinging above the pit. She reached out her mind to the spider there, wondering if it enjoyed what it saw, after all Mei was just another fly trapped in the web of spiders.

As the men bruised her flesh and broke her bones she wailed, screamed, and cried out for her mother. The last words on her lips were an ancient curse Nana had taught her. She felt the men lift her body and throw her into the pit before the blackness took hold.

Mei – Seconds Later

The darkness in Mei's mind was safe and inviting. "You stupid child. Never listened to your mama." Her mother called out. "I'm dead and you are dying. Who will give me the proper respect now?"

"Mama?" Mei saw her mother' grey as a ghost in her mind.

"Of course. Look at you. Allowing men to use you and throw you away. I thought you'd do better than me."

"I tried." Mei cried. In the corner something skittered and lurked. The spider, now larger than in life appeared before them.

"What is this?"

"You brought us both here, child." The spider whispered in a voice like her grandmother's. "Your dying words are the only thing that can save you now. But you must make a choice."

"What. What choice?" Mei wondered, though she knew well enough nothing was without a price. "I must go now." Mama stated as though she were off to the store, not whatever came next.

"No. Please stay."

"I've already given you my strength, child. There is nothing more I can do." Her mama faded as the spider hurried forward. Mei knew it was true, for without strength she'd have succumbed to the darkness.

"Now that we are alone I will ask you this, did you mean what you said to the men before you died?" The spider wondered.

"Those men do not know pain and suffering. They should." Mei felt conviction in her words and the fire of pain burned into an inferno of anger.

"Good. Now I can put you back together for a time. Once your revenge is complete the work will unravel. Do you understand?" Spider asked.

Mei knew what that meant. She would have time but only for the task at hand. The men who wronged her would suffer but when it was over she would perish. "I understand. Let me take my revenge."

Tommy – The Next Night

"Have you heard from Mei?" Tommy asked the following night when he returned to work. The tension was palpable, the men uneasy.

"No. Heard her mother died." Dan muttered, not lingering to talk. He looked over his shoulder and the smirk he wore faded to worry. Tommy tried talking to the other men but no one would answer his questions. Mei had punched into work the night before, but never clocked out and now she wasn't here.

Tommy looked over the line for any sign of her, a note or clue perhaps. At the end of the line the box of trimmings was empty. A knot formed in Tommy's stomach as he thought of the pit. He rushed from his corner towards the opposite side of the building. She'd emptied the box which meant she was at the pit. Tommy had only heard rumors, but he knew the men well enough to know they might do it again.

He stood at the edge of the pit looking down into it. The light had gone out overhead and no one bothered to change it. As ominous as the pit was with a little light now it was downright frightening. There was no body or any sign that something was dumped that should not be there. Without climbing in to search he couldn't be sure. He gazed into the shadows along the ceiling. 'Was that movement?' he wondered but blinked and it was gone.

"Tommy!" Dan called, "Get back to work." He scolded. Tommy turned to leave, watching as Floyd approached the pit to unload a box. He did not look at Tommy but peered straight ahead.

Mei

Mei watched Tommy from her shadowy perch on the ceiling. She hung there like a spider in a web, which she was. After waking from the nightmare she'd crawled to the ceiling and began to weave. Tommy was not one she wished revenge upon. She let him go along with the second man, it was too risky to pick him off with Tommy so close.

After the break she had her first chance to take revenge. The portly, bald man who'd held her down last night came into range. With surprising speed she launched down from the darkness, plucked him up and carried him away before the box he was holding could hit the floor. She whispered in his ears all the things he'd said to her the night he held her down. She wanted him to know she was causing his suffering.

She sank her fangs into his neck, paralyzing him, knowing he would be unable to move or scream. Then she began to peel the flesh from his bones, one layer at a time. When she was satisfied he'd suffered enough she wrapped him into a cocoon and strung him up.

Later as the men looked around for their coworker Mei watched and waited with the satisfaction of her first kill still fresh in her mind.

When Floyd returned she pushed him into the pit from behind. Scurrying down to join him she made quick work of binding his head so he couldn't call for help. Mei let him dangle while she watched him. She could see his silent screams.

Pat was her next victim, along with one whose name she didn't know. They came in together and she took a chance to capture them at once. She yanked the nameless man up into the rafters and bound him while Pat called out for him. After making work of his friend she hung upside down on the threads and crawled towards Pat. He looked up just as she struck him. His cries were lost in the noise and she hauled him up next to the others.

Mei did not wonder what became of her mother, or her sister. Nor did she worry what the authorities were thinking when they came to question her coworkers about her disappearance. By that time, several men were missing from the factory and the remaining men along with Tommy were questioned and let go.

Tommy

"Dan what aren't you telling me?" Tommy asked after the third man went missing. The police suspected foul play, considering all four worked together on the same shift, but no one was talking. Tommy, the only worker remaining with an alibi was not a suspect.

"Mind your own business Tommy." Dan replied.

"Where is Mei? What did you do and why are you all so scared?"

"Shut your mouth and do your job." Dan threatened. Tommy let it go but the questions still lingered. He knew for certain Mei had come to some untimely end and now the culprits were covering their trail.

He walked to the back room as the sun crested over the hills. The day shift was an hour out and he should be punching out and heading home. Still he lingered. "I wish I'd been here that night. I knew when Dan sent me to the other factory something was wrong. He said you weren't coming in. You would be out another day." Tommy felt the tears brim in his eyes but blinked them away. "Damnit Mei." He cursed.

She moved. It was subtle but enough to draw Tommy's eyes. He could not see her but this time he was prepared. He turned on the flashlight and searched the ceiling. As he scanned for the movement, always one step behind it, he saw the large bundles wrapped in cocoons made from the castoff threads below.

Then he saw her, or what she had become. He dropped the flashlight in his fright. "Don't be alarmed. I won't hurt you." The voice belonged to Mei but it was changed, full of sorrow and rage, the gentle rain, and the loud thunder.

"What...?" He started to speak then shook his head and groped for the flashlight. "Don't come any closer. Whatever you a..." His words died as he saw her in the full light of the factory. She'd moved with lightning speed and now stood before him.

"They abused me. They hurt me. I remain to take my revenge."

"But. How?" Confusion raced through Tommy's mind as he stared at the knitted woman and her strange new form. He looked away. The beautiful young girl Mei once was had become a horror. He could not stand to look at her knowing he failed.

"I'm sorry." He whispered.

"Go. Let me finish my work and I will be gone from here. Remember me as I was." She offered. Tommy rushed off; careful not to touch any part of this creature. He felt pity where he'd once held hope of asking her on a date.

Tommy called in sick the following week and when he returned the rope factory was shut down. "Police won't let us in." Dan puffed on a cigarette while leaning against his rust bucket of a truck.

"Thought you gave that up?" Their boss, Luke, commented, coming over to stand with them.

"So did I." Dan replied.

"I have to ask if either of you know what's going on here? Two more guys went missing last night. That's my entire overnight shift save the two of you." Luke looked from Tommy to Dan and back towards the building. Tommy cautioned a glance at Dan who shot him a dark look.

"Can't say as I understand it myself. Drugs maybe." Dan offered. "I know that girl was shifty. Maybe she got the others involved in something."

"Yeah but she was the first to go missing. The police asked me about that other woman, Tina, Tanya... whatever her name was that worked here five years ago. She disappeared as well didn't she." Tommy watched Dan put out the first cigarette and light another.

"I can't recall." Dan muttered. Luke walked away towards the cops while the men stood by watching. "Whatever you think you know zip it." He warned.

"I know a hell of a lot more than you'd like me to know. You are slime and whatever happens to you, you deserve it."

"Tommy, I don't know what you think-" Tommy cut him off with a glance towards the officers, taking an interest in Dan's heated words. He swallowed, threw his lit cigarette, and stalked off. Tommy followed. As they rounded the back of the building Tommy saw the door leading into the pit. A thought occurred to him so he led Dan closer to the door. While Dan lit another cigarette, Tommy took out his smart phone and pressed record, keeping the screen from Dan's view.

"It's not that I am angry at you. Couldn't you have let me in on it?"

"Why would we let you have any fun? Dan replied. "That little piece of ass wasn't enough for the six of us as it was.

"Yeah but you didn't have to send me away. Come on just tell me what it was like." Tommy encouraged him. He pretended to play a game on his phone while he waited for Dan. "I'm sure the other guys are locked up in a cell somewhere in police custody. Who's idea was it? Maybe you can cut a deal." Tommy offered. Still it seemed like Dan wouldn't take the bait.

Tommy, having no choice, nodded towards the door. "I know you left her in the pit. I found her. She's different but still alive. You should see for yourself."

Dan's eyes grew larger as fear filled his face. "She killed them, didn't she? Did you help her?"

"No. I didn't help her and I would have stopped you had I known. Now. Go see for yourself." He took a step forward as Dan took a step back. They neared the door this way. Dan opened it with shaking hands. It was silent inside. All the machines had been shut down.

Mei

Mei heard the noise outside and with it Tommy's voice. She listened and waited, hovering near the door. Above her the bundles were wrapped up tight, concealing the remains of her murderers. Only Dan remained.

Tommy, it seemed, was on her side. He had lured Dan into the area from the back. He stood in the doorway, the moonlight illuminating the near empty pit below. Only a few bits of thread remained. She whispered to Dan then.

"Come to apologize for what you've done?" She asked.

"What the hell? Is this a joke." Dan half turned to Tommy but his way was blocked by the young kid.

"Your friends await you. Come in and join them. I won't hurt you." Mei lied.

"No. Let me go."

"I recall saying the same thing that night. You didn't listen. Why should I?" The eerie disembodied voice of the girl sounded like a ghost from beyond the grave. Dan had seen enough movies to know this wouldn't end well. He started to call for help when he spotted her. She'd moved into a patch of light

Mei had been a petite girl with porcelain skin and raven hair. That was before they broke her body and left her to die. Dan could not move or speak as he looked at the monster before him. Her smooth ivory skin bore the colorings of bruises unable to heal. Her silky hair had been pulled out in clumps, leaving the raw red scalp oozing with infection. Various cuts had been stitched together with bits of multicolored thread, though many of those bulged at the seams with infected pus. Her limbs too were bound with the trimmings they cast off. The fibers binding her from hips to waist gave her midsection a swollen, bulbous appearance. Extra appendages like that of a spider jutted out, though these too appeared made of the materials that once filled the pit.

"I've been given a second life." She moved closer as she spoke to him. Dan could see her eyes now, where there had been two now eight sets watched him. Her missing and broken teeth were replaced with pincers. "The curse saved me and the spider stitched me back together. I am whole again so that I may take my revenge."

Dan's gaze followed Mei's as she looked upward, revealing the nest she'd created. Her killers bundled in neat packages. Tommy swore one of them moved.

"I swear we didn't mean to hurt you. It was only for a little fun. You were so timid we thought we could frighten you. Sure we took it too far." Dan admitted. "We didn't think you would die. It was only supposed to be sex but you fought us and well the guys got carried away." He stuttered his way through a confession but not one apology was given.

Dan was still looking up when Mei struck him. The blow sent him to his knees. Before he could move she bit his neck. "You do not know pain, but you will." She cried as the paralysis took hold.

Tommy watched her wrap threads around the body of the man as fast as any spider with a fly. Then she pulled him into the ceiling on her strings and plastered him there with the other men. The pain they felt in these cocoons made her suffering pale. She climbed back down a thread, lingering upside down over the now empty pit. Tommy still held his phone, recording the entire thing though he'd forgotten about it.

"What did you do to them?"

"They are alive and unable to move. The spider that saved me is taking care of their suffering, but they will not die if you help them."

"Mei. I'm so sorry I didn't save you." Tommy said again. Mei's gaze was full of longing and regret.

"I really liked you Tommy. Look after my sister would you?" She let go of the thread holding her up and fell into the pit below. She hit the bottom in an explosion of threads and trimmings. Tommy looked up to see black spiders crawling all over the cocoons. He could hear the muffled screams from within.

Tommy

The police could not explain much of what they found when they swarmed the building. Tommy alerted them that Dan confessed and entered the building through the back door. Tommy swore he tried to stop him.

When the police cleared the building to the pit it was empty. In the pit however, covered with a thin layer of cast off materials they found Mei, her body badly broken and decomposed for weeks. Overhead spiders crawled around six human size cocoons.

Tommy stood outside as they cut the men down and brought them out of the building. Unwrapping them the men were in various states of decay, parts of their limbs liquified while they were still alive. Dan was covered in a thousand spider bites and babbling incoherently.

None of the men survived, but their deaths were painful and their minds broken by nightmares of a girl they killed. Tommy never showed the footage to anyone, but years later it found its way to some internet site claiming the spider girl had killed the men. It was believed to be a hoax. Only Tommy knew the truth. He never harmed another spider again.

To the end of the world they heard her cry…
A single yelp and a single goodbye.

Aliens & Demons

I was and still often am terrified of grey-skinned, black eyed aliens. Watching the miniseries Taken with my husband helped cure me of some of those fears but it was my brother who helped those fears take root as a child. My father taught me that fear was a mindset and we could choose to be afraid or not. If I could look at something logically I was less afraid. The problem was I thought it mathematically impossible as a child that we were alone in the universe and therefore no amount of logic would quell my fear of aliens coming to take me away.

Ben

My sister Jessie hates aliens. She blames me. Of course it wasn't my fault that at a young age she couldn't handle looking at the stars and being told of the mysteries of space. All I said was that the aliens from TV shows would come take her away and she may never see her family again. That's what big brothers are for. Scaring our baby sisters is a genetic predisposition. We can't help it.

My uncle scared my mom with creepy crawly things, but my sister didn't seem to mind snakes and worms and spiders. She was terrified of the science fiction docudramas during the late Eighties. The ones which depicted dark eyed grey skinned alien life forms visiting our planet. I used what I had.

No one seemed to realize how terrified she was except me. It was something I enjoyed holding over her. Yes it may have been mean, and I did abuse the power a wee bit but it was all fun. I never thought anyone would be hurt by the pranks. Boy was I wrong.

Although her fear started young it was not until Jessie was fifteen that things took a disastrous turn. Three years older, I was heading off to college that fall, so as one last bonding moment I took her to the fair. Jessie was excited to play the midway games. She tried her hand at several, but it was my steady hand which won a prize of any stuffed animal. I could have picked the cute bears or tigers but my eyes landed on a bright green glow in the dark, black eyed alien. Perfect!

"That one." I exclaimed.

"No." Jessie cried. "Anything but an Alien."

"I won it for you." I said, as the man handed me the stuffed creature. I held it out to Jessie who refused to take it. My pretend pout was short lived and we continued our evening adventures.

That evening when Jessie was sleeping I put the stuffed animal in her room. Of course that was after I explained to my mother that it was Jessie's prize and she should make sure it's always in her room to remember me by. My mother did not know Jessie had an irrational fear response to all things alien. I'd seen her break down into a hysterical fit once when our friends, spotting some mysterious light in the sky started yelling for the "aliens" to come our way.

Jessie was in for a surprise when she woke to find the alien staring at her, all glowing and dead eyed. The next day she did not say a word to anyone. I didn't see the stuffed alien before I went off to college.

"I hate you." Jessie muttered into the phone. Our parents were out so I was stuck talking to her.

"Why?"

"Mom keeps putting the alien in my closet. Do you know what it is like to wake up and see that thing. It's horrible." She cried. I was laughing. I missed what she said next.

"You are afraid of a little stuffed animal?" I imagined her waking up seeing it at the foot of her bed and laughed a bit more.

"Bye." She hung up. I thought that would be the end of it, but a few weeks later my mother reported that she found the alien in my room and other strange places around the house, as if Jessie were trying to hide it.

"Do you know about this?" She asked. I feigned ignorance. Jessie would just have to learn to hide it better or get rid of it some other way.

"I remember when you were a kid someone gave you a demon stuffed animal for… I think it was your first Halloween. You hated that toy. You don't think Jessie dislikes this one do you?" Mom wondered.

"No. She loves it. She was holding it all night. She must carry it around the house and forget where she leaves it. You know how she can be." I offered. I had no way of knowing Jessie heard mom's share of the conversation that night.

Jessie

I loved my family, but my brother was obnoxious. Big brothers always are but sometimes I thought Ben took it to an extreme out of spite. He was the middle child. I'd had it with the aliens. I grew up learning there was nothing to be afraid of in the dark, that spiders were useful and wild animals were often more afraid of me. So I grew up fearless. Except when it came to aliens.

I hated aliens. Stories of abductions and strange lights in the sky worried me. Were they real? Fake? No one knew for certain and because there was no proof either way. I couldn't disbelieve without hard evidence. The unknown element of aliens created a sense of fear for me. If they were out there did they intend to harm me?

Ben had me believing that they in fact would harm me. It was years of phycological torture. The government could learn something from the abuse of older siblings against their younger, helpless counterparts. I had managed to keep my fear at bay for years now, until he won the stupid stuffed animal. Sure it was just a toy, but a creepy, glow in the dark menacing toy which my mother insisted on leaving in my closet at the foot of my bed every time she found it.

I had planned to destroy the toy but when I heard my mother talking about the Halloween toy I formulated a dark plan.

"Mom, do you know where I might find our baby stuff? I have a school project that requires some old photos."

"Sure. There are a few boxes in the basement and the rest in the attic. Do you want some help?" She offered. I declined stating I would start it that weekend.

On Saturday when the house was empty I began my hunt through boxes of pre-k stick figure drawings and old report cards. It was in the back of the attic where I found a box labeled 'baby to keep.' I undid the tape and found a box with special clothes and blankets. At the bottom there was a small, wrapped object. Unraveling the wrap I found what I was looking for.

The demon was a plush stuffed toy of the most hideous nature. No wonder he feared it. I closed the box back up and took the toy downstairs to my room. In the light it was worse than I'd first realized. On each side of the face four small eyes stared at me, like a crazed spider. The mouth was a toothy grin made of felt. Curled plastic horns sprouted from the head, and a barbed tail from the back. The tail was pointed plastic at the tip. It even had claws on the tips of the hands and feet in the same molded plastic.

Though I thought it was more devil than demon it was a dangerous child's toy that parents nowadays would protest, but it was what my brother was afraid of. The matted fur had a bad red dye job and over time faded to a rust color reminiscent of blood. I grinned as the evil plan twisted in my mind.

Ben

What happened next is a matter of some debate. There are those who say it would be impossible. It was the sleep deprived stress of an overworked college Freshman. No one believed Jessie could be capable of such madness and if it had happened to anyone else I too would share in the disbelief.

I woke up in the middle of the night on a Sunday to the sound of something hitting the door. Dorm life was chaotic, with students in the halls at random hours. Some drunk idiots probably banged against the door trying to find his room.

But then it happened again. I sat up, rubbed my eyes, and tried to focus on the source of the noise. I heard a scraping sound against the door. Glancing across the room I looked to see if my roommate heard the noise as well. A gentle snore emerged from his bed and I knew he was fast asleep.

Turning back to the door I could see the light from the hallway. Something blocked part of the light, perhaps a foot. I had the urge to throw something at the door but instead I laid down and tried to sleep.

The feeling of unease crawled across my brain like a spider stalking a fly. I was the fly. I listened, trying to steady my breathing which had become shallow. My heartbeat thumped against my chest, but soon that too slowed and I was lulled back into a deep sleep.

The nightmare began again. This time I was certain it was a dream because I couldn't move. The door to our dorm, which was locked in three places, opened. I remembered locking it before crawling into bed. A small shadow stretched across the floor before the door closed again, bringing the return of darkness. My brain was onto the next point of panic before it could fully register the last.

I blinked. Straining to hear the slightest noise I held my breath. Something scurried across the floor. Nails scraping across the linoleum. 'A mouse.' I thought. More like a rat guessing from the size. I shuddered. The blanket at my feet moved. Something tugged at it from below.

Still unable to move or wake myself I felt the panic build. Whatever it was had crawled onto the bed and now sat at my feet. I did not dare look. I screwed my eyes shut tight. Something touched my foot. My eyes popped open, an involuntary response. I tried to stop myself from looking towards the end of the bed. My eyes were drawn towards it unwillingly. There, atop my feet and crawling closer was no rat. It was a horrible tiny monster. Hideous fangs dripped saliva as it longed for flesh. Clawed fingers dug into my legs beneath the blanket as a forked tail swished back and forth behind it.

The demon from my childhood had returned. It was real. I screamed and flung the covers, jumping out of bed.

"Wha…" My roommate rose in alarm. I dashed across the room, flicked on the light, and found… nothing.

"Bad dream?" Roommate wondered. I searched under the bed, under the covers, in the closet but there was no sign of anything in the room.

"I thought there was a rat." I explained. I felt lame. My roommate gave me a strange nod and rolled back over to sleep. But sleep wouldn't find me that night. Or many nights after that.

I developed a bad habit for caffeine in any form, pills, energy drinks, soda. I had to stay awake for class and when I did fall asleep the demon found me. Several times I fell asleep without warning. The last time this happened before break the demon toy found me.

I was bound, unable to move. The horrendous beast was no tiny fiend, but now a raging entity standing seven feet tall. In hits clawed, gnarled hands it held a whip. The tips were shards of glass, a cat o' nine tails. He was skilled with the art of whipping. The first lash came with a sudden noise, the cracking, but his movement was subtle.

The pain was anything but subtle. The glass bit my flesh, sank in, and pulled back out with a yank of a single flourish. I howled in pain. The demon laughed. He whipped again, and again. Each time my blood splattered the room and my vision swam with crimson stars.

I was shaken awake, screaming in the lounge of my dorm floor. My books under my head where I'd been reading.

"Dude. You were screaming. Bad dream?"

"He's bleeding." Someone else said. I felt my shirt cling to my back. Abandoning my books I ran for my dorm room. The wounds were not deep, more superficial. But I had a sinking feeling that if I slept too long or too often the manifestation of my dreams would kill me.

Jessie

Ben arrived home for Thanksgiving looking like a zombie. Dark purple ringed his bloodshot eyes. I snickered. Seemed he was having trouble sleeping, though he wouldn't say why to my mother. I made a point not to be alone in the room with him so he couldn't bother me about it. I knew why he wasn't sleeping. I didn't care what they said about revenge, it was sweet and hilarious when extracted this way.

My grandmother said I'd been touched with a gift when I was a child, the ability to see other worlds. Maybe that is why aliens frightened me so much. But it did allow an old world magic to flow through me. I had sent the demon toy through my brother's dreams. The toy itself was hidden away in a place he'd never think to look. I took pride in my genius.

Thanksgiving morning when the adult men went out hunting and the adult women cooked a fantastic feast the children and teenagers were left to their own devices. That is when Ben cornered me.

"What did you do to me?" His eyes blazed with anger.

"No... nothing." I feigned.

"Liar." He'd followed me into the back yard. "I have scratches on my legs and torso to prove it." We had to stay out of the woods so I made my way to the empty barn and sat with my book in the hay loft. He snatched the book out of my hands. Tossing it aside he reached down and pulled me to my feet. Shaking me until my teeth clattered he muttered threats and payback.

"Payback? That's what this is. You tortured me for years with stories of aliens and then convinced mom to put that stupid thing in my room all the time. Do you know how much sleep I've lost because of that damn toy."

"So you somehow animate my stuffed animal and get it to stalk me?" I giggled. Ben let me go.

"I'm not practicing voodoo or dark magic. It's not real Benny boy. It's all in your head."

"I told you not to call me that." He grimaced. He turned his back on me and looked out the loft door onto the house below. "So this is revenge for my own stupid pranks?"

"One good turn..." I chuckled.

"I need you to stop it."

"Only if you do. Help me destroy the alien and I will stop your nightmares."

"Deal." Ben agreed. I made him pinky promise.

Ben

I made Jessie promise to bring the stupid demon toy with her, but when she followed me outside after dark she only carried the alien animal instead. Before I could ask her about it, she dashed off up the hill and into the pine forest behind our house. Armed with a flashlight, propane torch and lighter fluid I was prepared to destroy the alien. I'd hoped to destroy my own demon in the process. She stopped and I recognized the familiar clearing. A ring of stones around a shallow hole were blackened from years of use. In the trees to our left, though I couldn't see it, was a platform we built as a fort. We'd camped here a few times as kids. She tossed the alien in the fire pit.

"You said you'd bring the demon."

"Just light it and watch." She stated. I humored her and doused the toy with the fluid.

"Stand back." I warned. She took a few steps back. I flicked the torch on and set the flame to the glow in the dark alien. The synthetic fur covered in fuel caught fire in a dramatic flash of flames.

It blazed strong before dying down and settling into a red-orange blaze. As the body of the alien melted away I caught sight of a familiar horror. Inside the alien the demon toy from my childhood rose like a chest bursting plushy.

"What the-" I stumbled back. An inhuman screech and inorganic hum began to fill the clearing as the two toys melted into one and burned to a pile of ash. Thick black smoke rose from them, releasing whatever hold they had upon us. When the fire died to smoldering embers I found my voice.

"You hid it inside the alien?" I asked Jessie.

"I thought it was the last place you'd look for it." She grinned. "Now, promise me no more aliens."

"Only if you promise to keep demons out of my nightmares." I agreed.

"Deal." We covered the remains of the firepit with dirt to be sure it was completely out and made our way back to the house. Jessie took off running shouting something about the last one home was rotten. I let her win, after all what else are big brothers for?

Darkest Hour

2020 started out with such promise. Then it all went downhill, right! When I found out that Halloween 2020 would be on a Saturday, during a blue moon on the eve of daylight savings time I had to write a story about it.

The darkest hour on Halloween seemed like the perfect time to partake in mystical practices, even if the sky was light as bright as day. We decided to meet up in the old graveyard on the hill above town. The open field was ringed with tall oaks and maples, a few pines, and crabapples. The only time anyone came to this place was to learn the history of the smallpox outbreak that claimed the lives of the poor souls buried on this hill.

Brett, Caleb, Lisa, Jill, and I had spent our younger years dressing up in themed costumes and roaming the wild streets of our quaint village, pillaging the neighbors for candy! This year the town limited trick-or-treats to children under sixteen. At the cusp of adulthood they preferred us older kids to find our own kind of trouble.

We settled for raiding our parents' alcohol stash weeks ago, hiding the goods and planning for the best Halloween in our short lives. This year it fell on Saturday with a full blue moon and the end of daylight savings time. We would have an extra hour for our shenanigans.

I was the only one without an official curfew, my parents wanted the where and why of it. I told them we were hanging out at a friend's house. The others did the same, hoping our parents wouldn't check on us. No one expected us before 9 the next morning.

I arrived at the cemetery first, after parking my car down the hill and walking up the paths. Lisa and Jill arrived together. They had sexy makeup and skimpy costumes; the way girls always seemed to do when they grew up. Brett and Caleb arrived a bit later. We all brought alcohol and cracked a few beers before hitting the harder stuff.

"So Jeff, what's the deal with your sister?" Caleb asked as I watched Jill and Lisa dance to imaginary music.

"Hands off." I replied. "She's too young and innocent for you."

"Yeah, not like them." Brett whispered in a hushed tone. We chuckled, causing the girls to turn their attention back to us. Jill pouted but Lisa strutted over and stood over me as I sat with my back to the cemetery fence.

"What's so funny?" She said. I grinned up at her as she stood there. Before long she grinned and sat down on my lap facing me.

"If you won't tell me I will find out myself." She dared. Reaching next to me where our bags were piled together she pulled out a cloth wrapped object. It looked about the size of a laptop, but when she slid the fabric cover off I could see the wood grains and fire burned markings.

"No!" Jill jumped back. Brett looked just as concerned. They were from religious families and believed in everything evil.

"No way am I doing that." Caleb tried to bow out.

"Oh come on. It's just a talking board." Lisa reached into the bag and pulled out an ornate planchette. Instead of the typical heart shape this one was carved from the branches of a tree, shaped like a hand with a finger pointing to the symbols on the board.

"I'm game." I grinned. "If they others are too scared then I will just have to protect you." I joked, wrapping my arms around Lisa, and blowing her hair away from her ear. "The spirits will never take you from me." She shivered, flashed me her sexiest smile and scooted over so we were side by side. She set the talking board on one of the small flat stones in the graveyard and looked at the others.

"Look if you wimp out, I'll take Jeff and all the alcohol here and we will find our own party. It's almost 1. We've only got an hour before the clocks fall back and I'm due home." She had a way of staring others down. I knew Jill would cave if the boys stayed. I gave them the 'dude, don't chicken out now' look and watched as their resolve caved.

"I guess so." Jill mumbled when Caleb and Brett moved closer.

Once we were all circled around the board we placed two fingers on each groove of a knuckle. "What were the boys laughing about?" Lisa asked in a commanding voice. It carried through the quiet woods. The hoot of an owl called back as something scampered in the dry leaves.

We all held our breath as the planchette began to move.

"S." We read in unison, "E." Jill dropped her fingers.

"Really guys. Like we didn't know you were thinking about that. When aren't you."

"Okay fine." I spoke up. "Ask it something else?" I dared Jill. She pouted again, her red lips plump and kissable. I grinned.

"Fine." She agreed and we all placed our fingers back on the designated spots. "Is Jeff a virgin?" She giggled. I choked and pulled my hands back. Behind us something snapped a branch and I jumped.

"Now who's afraid." Brett teased. I punched his shoulder. "Ow. Jerk." He shot back.

"Okay be serious. I want to ask it some real questions. Everyone knows Jeff screwed Coach Marie in the 9th grade." Lisa mouthed off. It was a rumor I'd never bothered to quash. After all Coach Marie was a college intern who coached basketball my 9th grade year and the hottest teacher any of us could recall. I arrived early to practice a few times to up my game, but everyone thought I had other reasons. Why admit I was a virgin when I had a reputation as a bad boy.

"So what do you want to ask?" Jill was hesitant. She shivered as a cold breeze carried dead oak and maple leaves into the air sweeping across the cemetery. We took our places for the third time.

"I seek the dead buried beneath our feet. Are any of their spirits present tonight?" Lisa asked. We all watched the planchet. At first it remained still. Then the finger moved and pointed to 'yes.' Lisa gave a short screech of pleasure and continued with her questions.

Did they have a name? Elijah. Was Elijah alone? No. Where were the others? All around us. How many of you are there? At this time, the planchet pointed to the infinity symbol and Jill dropped her hands again.

"That's it. Enough of this. I don't want any part of it." She turned to look at Brett who stood and pulled her to her feet.

"I'll take her home. Coming Caleb?"

"Yeah" He joined them, reaching for his backpack. "Sorry guys." He frowned as Lisa glared at them. I shrugged.

"Guess it's just us baby." I grinned at Lisa and pulled her closer.

"Yeah." She watched as the others headed back down the trail. A shadow crossed the full moon overhead at that moment casting us into darkness. The wind picked up to a gale strength rushing through the pine boughs overhead and scattering leaves around us. Jill's scream filled the air as the moonlight returned. She was standing at the trail she'd just gone down, but she was looking behind us. I turned to see a figure looming tall. The man stood over six feet easy. Lisa couldn't move before his hand closed over her hair and dragged her backwards into the shadows.

"Let her go." I yelled trying to follow. I stumbled over a headstone. Behind me Jill was screaming.

"What's going on?" Caleb yelled from somewhere down the hill. Brett remained silent. I figured it was their version of an elaborate prank to scare us. I scrambled back to my feet and took off up the hill. I could hear Lisa struggling with someone but as I neared the forest fell silent.

"Guys? If it's a joke it isn't funny." I called out. No one answered.

Turning back I saw a woman standing in the cemetery with her back to me. Her blond hair was pulled up, but Lisa's had been down. Still it wasn't hard to put her hair in a ponytail. Before I could take a step towards her she flew through the fence, her body passing without breaking the wood, and threw herself at Jill.

The scream died on Jill's lips as the spirit disappeared into her body. Her face twisted in pain, the tears falling silent down her cheeks. Within seconds her skin began to change, as a rash formed on her face and down her arms. I stepped back. She coughed and shivered as the phantom left her body and rushed down the hill out of my sight. I ran to Jill, scaling the fence in time to watch her fall to the ground. Her body spasmed as she coughed up dark liquid. I peered down as the moon illuminated her face.

To my horror the skin was blistered up in what I could only guess was smallpox. But that wasn't possible. The dead were buried long ago and the disease with them. We'd been up here a hundred times. Plus it didn't progress that fast.

Still as I stood there, Jill's body seized and she collapsed and stilled. With a final cough she died.

"Brett. Caleb. Lisa?" I screamed and called for my friends. I ran down the hill towards the guys.

Caleb ran at me, his face also covered in a similar familiar rash. I side stepped and watched him run into a tree. He stumbled and fell and was as good as dead.

"Jeff. What the hell was that thing?" Brett asked running onto the trail. "It went inside Caleb."

"I think it's a ghost with smallpox. Jill is dead. He will be soon enough. Come on they took Lisa."

"They, what do you mean?"

"Some man. He was tall. He pulled her like a ragdoll." As if on cue Lisa's tortured scream filled the air. The pain and anguish in her cry propelled me headlong up the hill. We passed the cemetery running deeper into the woods behind it. I'd never been this far before. Behind me Brett cursed as he tripped. I didn't stop to check on him. Lisa was my focus now.

I broke through a patch of pines into a clearing. There, bathed in the light of the blue moon six figures stood in a circle. Their skin and clothes appeared pale and translucent, the way you would expect a ghost in a cheesy horror film to look. In the center of them Lisa was laying on her back held down by some unseen force as the figures closed in. I circled to the left to see if I could come at them another way. As I did the tall man who'd taken Lisa appeared. He was kneeling before her. Sickness overcame me. I turned and lost the contents of my stomach. She screamed as they tore at her flesh. Behind me Brett laid a hand on my shoulder and yanked me to my feet.

"She's lost. Come on." He whispered. We rushed back into the forest, but I knew we weren't alone.

Elijah said their numbers were infinite. The souls of every person lost in this valley roamed the hills tonight.

I hit the button on my watch, illuminating the time. Ten to two. The clocks would reset in another ten minutes. Lisa wouldn't make it home in time for curfew, or ever again. I was lost in my own head about the deaths of my friends that I lost track of Brett. He made a choking sound ahead of me, as if his air were cut off. He'd stopped moving. When I reached him he turned and held his neck, the blood gushing out from a deep gash. The cemetery was straight ahead so I veered to the right, leaving Brett and the others behind. As I passed the cemetery I tripped. Cursing I looked back to see a small rectangular headstone jutting up from the ground. I hadn't known any stones were outside of the fence. I tried to scramble away and stand but something held my leg. I was stuck.

No matter how hard I tugged I felt as though I was being pulled further back towards the stone. A hundred hands pulled at me, tearing my jeans, and raking my skin with sharp fingernails. It burned like hot irons as my skin blistered and tore. I screamed and fought but the hands continued to pull me down. My feet sank beneath the grave dirt, followed by my legs. I was chest deep, clawing the ground and crying out for help as the alert on my phone beeped to inform me of daylight savings. The clocks rolled back an hour just as I took one last breath and screamed. Grave dirt filled my mouth as it all went black.

I opened my eyes in time to hear Lisa's voice utter familiar words. "I seek the dead buried beneath our feet. Are any of their spirits present tonight?"

"No" I shouted and pulled my hands away.

"What the hell, Jeff?" Lisa yelled. To our astonishment the planchette moved to signify we were not alone.

"We're all gonna die." I scrambled to my feet and took off into the woods. I ran into something solid though nothing blocked my path. I was lifted off my feet by invisible hands. They wrapped around my neck choking the air from me. I gasped for a breath but none would come and I blacked out before death overwhelmed me.

"Are any of the spirits present tonight?" Lisa finished saying when I opened my eyes again. As the planchette moved a guttural moan escaped my lips. "Jeff, you're pale. What's wrong?"

"I've done this before. We're gonna die again and again." I muttered, before inspiration hit. While no one was touching the board I asked, "Are we dead?" We watched the planchette move of its own volition. Yes.

"Not funny Jeff." Jill was on her feet now.

"No it's not. We're already dead." I watched as my friends gathered their belongings and stalked into the night. I waited as I heard their screams. They ran in pandemonium. Each of them faced a brutal death over and over. I sat as the hands reached out from the graves and dragged me under. There was no use fighting when I knew the next time I opened my eyes it would start all over again. We died in the darkest hour and as the clocks rolled back we relived the hour of our death over and over again.

Eyes

Your eyes hold secrets only the sun does know.
Tears of pain linger there.
The moon bows her head low
as you mourn in the shadows.
Stars stop twinkling as you look up to them without a twinkle in your eye.
The sunrise is not reflected in your dark eyes.
Eyes of mystery.
Eyes that soak up the sun.

Royâ

Royâ is Persian (Farsi) for Dream. Dreams often make some of the best stories, if one can remember them the next day. Fortunately for me I am a lucid dreamer and it is rare for my dreams to fade before I can write down the gritty details. It is fun to take a dream and turn it into stories. It is only in the past few years I've opened myself up to the dark, twisted tales that haunt my dreams.

I always thought I was a bit different from the other girls. It's not to say I was conceited but I knew I was important. It was a feeling deep inside that something would happen to lead me to my destiny. It was far from my mind as I walked past the old farmhouse as I did every day.

My mind was on getting home where my mother waited for me. I was used to seeing the haggard woman, aged far beyond her years as she yelled at her children. I had asked her once why she forced her children to stack and place the colored rocks into giant symbols. The question led to her going on for over an hour. The lengthy explanation could be summed up in four simple words; to ward off evil. I'd avoided her after that.

The woman cried out and I looked up, startled by the new sound. The children screamed. I blinked. The sky turned blood red. Not streaks of colors at sunset, but a uniform red the color of crimson rust. Before I could ask her anything the woman ran for her house, gathering her children. She continued screaming. Her words were incoherent to my ears. Darkness spread from the horizon on a rush of wind. The woman and her children stop as the lights in their home blink out.

Embers fall like fiery raindrops, a torrent of hot flakes. They burn everything they touch, except me. I let them wash over my skin, holding my hand out in awe as warmth spreads through my body. Nearby the woman and her children turn to dust. It blows away on the wind. I watch with morbid fascination and a twinge of disbelief. People don't vanish into dust.

My thoughts turn to my mother. She was waiting for me. Worry and fear wash over me, leaving a cold sweat on my skin, despite the earlier warmth. I began to run, picking up speed with a thought. I've never run this fast in my life. The familiar street passed by in a blink and yet I was able to process the changes. Cars stalled in the middle of the street. Traffic and streetlights have gone dark. Houses empty, the front doors still open as if someone had been entering them. I dodged around a car. I pushed another one to the side with my mind. Superpowers. Not what I expected, but I wouldn't complain. I was alive.

I knew something was wrong the moment I turned up the driveway to our house. A small, secluded lot surrounded by trees blocked our house from the road. A dark energy radiated from my house. I slowed as I reached the front door.

"You can't have her." My mother was pleading with someone. I could hear her shrill voice before I opened the door. I could not hear the response that caused my mom to sob. I opened the door to the kitchen.

"Mom." I called out.

"Ah, it seems she's home after all. Come, let us greet Anahita. It is time she meets Ahriman."

"Don't call her that." My mother hissed. I had no time to think about their exchange before the source of my mother's anguish entered the kitchen. She was not what I expected.

She was ancient but carried herself with dignified grace, the way one expected a Queen might appear. Her presence filled the room and I gasped for breath as if she took all the air.

Covered in dark furs and deep silks and dripping with jewels the effect was beautiful and dangerous. Horns peeked out from her dark gray coif.

"Mom, what's going on?"

"My dear, aren't you lovely." The woman approached me; her hand raised to stroke my cheek. I pulled away. "Now, now. That's no way to treat your kin." I looked from this woman to my mom and back. "You're not family." I spat. "The world's going to hell out there Mom." I looked at my mother. "People are dying."

"As will your mother if you do not respect me, child. You have no choice. You will come with me. This is your fate." What she said made no sense but the elderly woman headed for the back door.

"Ana, you must go with her. There is so much I want to tell you but there is no time. You have to leave me."

"No. If I have to go you are coming with me. I'm not leaving you here."

"Impossible."

"Please." I begged. Outside the land shook as a horrendous noise rose from the ground itself.

"Very well." She agreed. She will not thrive where we are going. Only you will." She opened the door and stepped out. The landscape had changed from the beautiful tree lined street to a barren, windswept hellscape. She walked out and motioned for us to follow. I gripped my mother's hand and we trail behind her.

"You may call me Mâdarbozorg.[1]" The woman stated. "When we arrive at his house you will refer to him as Lord or Sir. You will treat him with utmost respect. You will know your place."

"What is going on." I begged them to tell me. "Mom, you know where she is taking us. Don't you." My mother didn't speak, but she nodded.

---

[1] Persian word for Grandmother.

As we walked the air warmed and the wind swept across the land carrying a biting sand with it. Before long, hills of obsidian rose beside us and we entered the haven of a valley. At the end of the valley stone steps rose high above the nearest hill and atop the mountain of obsidian a crimson hued citadel gleamed in the raw light.

"You are the seventh daughter to walk this path." Mâdarbozorg told me. She appeared to glide along the path. "I bought each of them here. Some by choice, and others by force. You are the first to bring a mortal with you."

"She's my mother."

"Yes and my daughter, in a way. You see I am the birth of your line, child. Each mother shares the story with her daughter on the day of their granddaughter's birth, until one is born who will start the cycle again. That one is you."

"She speaks the truth." My mother told me, squeezing my hand tight. "I wished it didn't have to be you."

"I don't understand."

"You will."

We had reached the stairs and I stared up the steep incline with trepidation but also a deep curiosity. My mother and Mâdarbozorg waited at the bottom as I started my climb. They did not follow. I did not stop.

The crimson stone up close was streaked with black, red obsidian was thought to be rare, but wherever we were it made up the entire castle before me. The doors opened on their own and I turned back for a moment. The two women followed but at a slow pace.

I took a deep breath and entered. The foyer was massive, the ceiling stretching stories overhead, where silks flowed down on either side. As tall as it was, the room was twice as long. At the end of the room a throne sat overlooking the scene.

I couldn't call it man on the throne, but he was what I would imagine a devil might look like. He was handsome of face, and his body was that of a man but cloven hooves and satyr legs completed the look. "Welcome Doxtar[2]." He called out. "Come kneel before me." I walked up to him but I refused to kneel. I stood tall.

"Tell me what this is about."

"You are a bold one. Feisty. Not like your predecessors at all." He scowled. "You will obey me in my kingdom."

"Not until you tell me what I'm doing here and why the world was destroyed." I demanded. As I neared him I could see his red eyes. "I'm in hell and you're Lucifer." His laughter surprised me.

"The tales your humans tell." He looked behind me where my kin joined us. "Have you told her nothing."

"We've tried but she will not listen." Mâdarbozorg said.

---

[2] Persian word for Daughter.

"You will listen now. For eighteen millennia the world has endured and I will not see the cycle broken by an insolent child."

"Eighteen?" I marveled. Humanity had not lived that long. "What are you talking about?"

"In the beginning your stories talk of darkness and light. The reality is that Mâd and I struck a bargain in that time. She had a daughter, beautiful, fair, and full of light. I had a son, dark and cunning."

I listened to him but I had turned to watch my mother. She knew the story; I could see it in her eyes.

"We both wished control to rule, our battle for supremacy was long and heated." Mâdarbozorg spoke from behind me. "It was when our children met and fell in love that the solution presented itself. I would live in my kingdom, he in his and together we would watch the mortal realm. My daughter and his son would wed. They would rule in his kingdom for a thousand years, then in my kingdom for another thousand. After that time they would return to the mortal world and be born and reborn among the mortals for another thousand years."

"This has happened six times before. You, Anahita are the seventh bride."

"The hell I am." I spat. His laughter echoed again.

"You can make this easy on yourself or you can choose to be difficult but the result will be the same. You will marry, you will bear a son who will be slain by your betrothed, then you will leave for the next kingdom where you will bear a daughter. She will betray you and at her hand you will return to the mortal world to start again." I ran to my mother and hugged her.

"Why didn't you tell me any of this."

"It was not time. I would tell you when you bore a daughter, I never thought you'd be the one."

"But I am." I cried.

"Then you must face this with dignity, daughter. It is your fate. You are Anahita the immaculate. You will marry Ahriman and rule. This is your fate." My mother hugged me but pulled away too quick for me. I wanted her to comfort me but I knew that was beyond her. We were both resigned to our fate.

"Go prepare. I will send her along." Cem instructed the women. They turned and left the room. "Now. I do not tolerate disrespect."

"It seems you need me." I found my voice again and my attitude.

"Tonight you and Ahri will be one."

"Have you ever heard the Charlie Daniels song about you?" I wondered. He slammed his fist on the arm of his throne and fire erupted from his fingers.

"You will do well not to anger me. You are immortal from the moment you and Ahri wed. You may have a purpose but I can cause you pain unlike you've ever known. Now go." He waved me away.

I turned and followed the way my mother had walked off. As I traveled down a wide hall it was decorated with magnificent trinkets from the various ages of humanity.

I heard voices down the corridor but stopped at an open door. The hall was filled with six massive paintings. I wandered in and looked at the first painting. The couple was familiar to me, a version of myself in demonic form.

I did not realize another figure was in the room until I heard him clear his throat. Without turning I knew the energy pouring off him. I stared at the demonic man in the painting and knew this was Ahriman, my betrothed.

My heart became light and full at the same time as memories of his face, his voice, his touch returned to me. I turned and peered upon a man as human as me. "Salam ātashé del-am.[3]" He said. His voice was soft and sultry. I could smell his cologne, leather, musk, and pine. "You still smell of lavender, linen and honey." His words mirrored my thoughts.

"Sobh bekheyr nooré cheshm-am.[4]" He called me the fire of his heart and he was the light of my eyes. The endearing terms in the ancient language were the first we spoke to each other every time we met.

"How I've missed you." He crossed the room to me. I understood because although in my human life I did not remember him, the moment we were in the same room together our souls united and our memories flooded back. He took me up in his arms and held me close. I breathed him in and felt the warmth radiating off his skin.

As strange as the day had been and all that I have learned I felt calm in his arms. He was my safety; I was his strength. For every thousand years we spent apart we had two thousand more joined together. In his arms I was home.

---

[3] Persian "Fire of my heart."
[4] Persian "Light of my eyes."

Made in the USA
Middletown, DE
03 October 2022